Hannah's Hope

THE RED GLOVES STORIES

Hannah's Hope

KAREN KINGSBURY

Guideposts

NEW YORK

Copyright © 2005 by Karen Kingsbury

Published by Guideposts a Church Corporation
39 Old Ridgebury Road, Suite 27
Danbury, CT 06810
Guideposts.org

This Guideposts edition is published by special arrangement with Hachette Book Group.

Printed in the United States of America
10 9 8 7 6 5 4 3

Cover by W Design Group, LLC.
Typeset by Aptara, Inc.

To . . .

Donald, my Prince Charming

Kelsey, my precious daughter

Tyler, my beautiful song

Sean, my wonder boy

Josh, my tender tough guy

EJ, my chosen one

Austin, my miracle child

And God Almighty, the author of life, who has—for now—blessed me with these.

ACKNOWLEDGMENTS

$\mathcal{A}$ special thanks to Rolf Zettersten, Leslie Peterson, Andrea Davis, Lori Quinn, Jennette Merwin, Preston Cannon, and everyone at Warner Faith who helped make this Red Gloves novel possible.

Also, thanks to my agent, Rick Christian, president of Alive Communications. Rick, you continue to amaze me, leaving me blessed beyond words. Thank you for keeping my family life and my faith as your utmost concern.

I couldn't complete a book without help from my husband and kids, who know what it is to eat tuna sandwiches and cheese quesadillas when I'm on deadline. Thanks for always understanding! I cherish every minute of our family time!

The work of putting together a book doesn't take place without other people picking up the slack in my life. A heartfelt thanks goes to my mother and assistant, Anne Kingsbury, and to assistants Katie Johnson and Nicole Chapman. Also thanks to Aaron Hisel for your work with Tyler, and to the Shaffers and Heads and Weils, and to Kira Elam and Tricia Kingsbury for helping out with rides when I'm on deadline.

Prayer is a crucial part of taking a book from its original idea to the written page. So, thanks to my prayer warriors—Ann Hudson, Sylvia and Walt Walgren, Sonya Fitzpatrick, Teresa Thacker, Kathy Santschi, the Chapmans, the Dillons, the Graves, and countless readers, friends, and family who lift my writing ministry to our Lord on a daily basis. I couldn't bring you these books without that type of support. Thank you!

Thanks also to those who keep me surrounded by love and encouragement. These include my extended family, my church friends, the parents on our various soccer, baseball, and basketball teams, and the wonderful friends who make up our Bible study group and closest relationships. You know who you are—you are wonderful! I love you all!

Finally, a humble thanks to the men and women of the U.S. Armed Forces, especially Air Force reservist Jonathan Vansandt. My family and I completely support your work overseas across the world—particularly the efforts in Iraq and Afghanistan. If you are one of these, please let me know. I love hearing from my readers, but especially I love hearing how these stories are encouraging you. Your sacrifice is immeasurable. You remain in our prayers and thoughts as you carry out your mission. Because of you, I have the freedom to write books that give glory to Jesus Christ.

Thank you isn't nearly enough.

Hannah's Hope

PROLOGUE

*H*annah Roberts was late for lunch. Again.
Her backpack was on a roller board, and
she pulled it as she darted down the hallway of
the music wing at TJ Prep, a private school for kids in
Washington, D.C.'s politically elite. Hannah had gone
here since sixth grade. As a freshman, she knew her way
through the halls as well as she knew her own house. She
tore into the commons area and bolted by the glass-
walled administrative offices, past the storied brick fountain at the front entrance. A bronze plaque read,
*"Bethesda, Maryland Welcomes You to Thomas Jefferson College
Preparatory School for the Leaders of Tomorrow."*

No doubt about that. A number of politicians,
lawyers, and international ambassadors had made their
way through TJ Prep. Hannah didn't care much about
that. Right now all she wanted was lunch. If she hurried,
she might still make it.

1

She burst through the lunchroom doors, her backpack flying along behind her. Several hundred students milled about, eating cheeseburgers and fries or sipping on pop cans while they caught up on the latest gossip. Most of the guys were gathered around a baseball game playing on the eight-foot flat-screen television at the center of the room. There was a line at the automatic teller machine in the corner, same as always, and a few stragglers remained at each of the food court windows.

There was still time.

Hannah tugged on her blue-plaid skirt and adjusted her white blouse as she rushed toward the Salad Sensation line. If she didn't eat now, she wouldn't have another chance until late that evening. Cheerleading practice went until five, and after that yearbook had a committee meeting until seven. By the time her driver picked her up, she'd barely have a minute for dinner before her dance instructor came at eight.

On her way to the salad window, two of her cheerleading friends approached her. "Hannah, you're so bomb!" Millie tapped her shoulder with her fingertips. "Where did you get that blouse? Bloomingdale's?"

"Saks." Hannah kept walking, but she smiled at her friends over her shoulder. "Save me a spot at the table."

"Save you a spot?" Kathryn put her hands on her hips. "Lunch is over in nine minutes. You'll never get here on time."

"I know." Hannah was next up. "Save me a spot anyway."

The girls looked put out. They hated when Hannah stayed late in choir and missed most of lunch. But they shrugged off their frustration and returned to their table.

It took Hannah three minutes to get her salad, and then, still rushing, she joined her friends. "Okay," she was out of breath. "What's up?"

"You won't believe it." Millie leaned low over the table, her voice little more than a whisper. "Brian—you know Brian, the senior in my algebra class—he came by my house the other day." She squealed. "Hannah, he wants to go out!"

"Really?" Hannah took a huge bite of salad. It didn't keep her from talking. "I thought you couldn't date a senior."

"I can't." Millie grinned. "My parents think he's a junior."

"Yikes." Hannah took another bite. "When they find out, you'll be grounded until summer."

"So?" Millie made a brushing gesture with her hands. "My dad's gone till then, anyway. He'll never know." She raised her shoulders a few times and glanced at the others. "Besides, nothing ever happens when I'm grounded. My parents always forget about it."

Kathryn finished her pop and pushed her can to the middle of the table. "My parents took my cell away, which stinks. Just because I'm getting a D in English." She exhaled hard, and her frown became the beginning of a grin. "But at least I don't get grounded."

"Yeah." Hannah took another two bites. She lived with her grandmother in The Colony, the enclave for D.C.'s wealthiest families. Whatever she wanted, she got. She could stay out late, date whomever, and she never lost her cell or her privileges. Not that she took advantage of the situation. She was too busy to get in trouble.

"You're blowing me off tonight." Kathryn plopped her elbows on the table and stared at Hannah. "You have yearbook." She made a face. "Frank Givens in Biology told me."

"Uh-oh." Hannah downed another bite of salad and grabbed her Palm Pilot from her Coach purse. A few key taps and she had her schedule up. "Yep. Yearbook five to seven." She would call for a ride after that. Her grandmother had a full-time driver, Buddy Bingo, a retired Navy guy. Buddy was available whenever Hannah needed him. She took another bite of salad and then scrolled down. "You're right." She looked up at Kathryn. "We were supposed to study."

"That's what I'm saying." Kathryn gave an exaggerated sigh. "We planned it a week ago."

"I remember." Hannah raked her hand through her thick, dark hair. "Give me a minute." A few more taps on her Palm. "Okay, how about six-thirty tomorrow after cheer practice? Dance classes are at eight this week." She found Kathryn's eyes again. "That gives us ninety minutes."

Before Kathryn could answer, two guys—a blond and a freckle-faced brunet—walked up. Both were juniors on the debate team, sons of senators. The blond took a step closer. He wore his usual cocky smile, the one that convinced so many of her friends to fall at his feet. "How's TJ's finest freshmen?"

"Well," Hannah lowered her chin and raised her brow at the boy. She wasn't interested, so why not have a little fun? "We're *fantastic*." She raised her voice above the conversations and clanking lunch trays in the cafeteria. In a school marked by money and madness, Hannah Roberts was one of the wealthiest, most prestigious girls on campus. There was no shortage of interested guys. "The question isn't how are the finest freshmen, but why the jerky juniors care?"

"Nice." The blond was unfazed. His grin crept a little higher into his cheeks. "Nothing gets to you, does it, Hannah Roberts?"

"Not much." She gave a practiced little wave to the guys. "See you around."

The bell rang before they could answer. The blond cocked his head. "Give me a call when you want a real man, Hannah."

"Okay." She took a long sip of water. "If I run across any, you'll be the first to know."

They walked away, Freckle Face laughing at Blondie.

Hannah chuckled, took the last two bites of her salad, stood, and tossed the plate into the nearest trashcan. Millie and Kathryn took up their places on either side of her.

"I can't believe you did that!" Millie's eyes were wide. "That was Jaden Lanning!"

"So?" Hannah picked up her pace. "I can't stand him." She rolled her eyes. "He thinks he's every girl's gift. Besides, I don't have time for guys."

"You don't have time for us, either." Kathryn hugged her books to her chest. She was doing her best to keep up as they maneuvered their way through the halls to their next class—a speech course, the only one they all shared. Kathryn blew at a wisp of her bangs. "Ever think about slowing down?"

"Never." Hannah's answer was even quicker than her pace. "I like staying busy."

"All right." They reached the classroom door and Kathryn lowered her voice to a whisper. "I just wish I knew what you were running from."

Hannah didn't answer. Already the conversation was too close for comfort. She gave her friend a smile that said she was finished talking. Then she made her way to her desk.

Her speech today was on the challenges of international politics—a topic normally reserved for juniors and seniors. But Hannah handled it like a master, no trouble. She could've given the talk without a bit of research. International politics was her parents' life.

❧

*A*fter school she led the cheerleaders in a new dance routine, one the cheer coach had asked her to create. "You're a better dancer than me, Hannah. Would you mind?"

"Not at all," Hannah had told her. Every challenge was a reason to keep going.

By five o'clock the squad had the dance down. Hannah grabbed her duffel bag and her roller backpack and sprinted across campus to the yearbook room. It was seven-thirty before she called Buddy for a ride. She must've looked exhausted because when he pulled up he gave her a worried frown.

"Runnin' on empty again, Miss Hannah?" He caught her look in the rearview mirror.

"A little." She smiled back.

Some days she spent more time talking to Buddy Bingo than anyone in her family. That wasn't saying much. Most of the year, the mansion she lived in was empty, home to just her and her grandmother.

Her father was the U.S. ambassador to Sweden, a former senator well known in the highest political circles. Her mother kept his social calendar, but for the past year she'd worked some at the embassy, serving as liaison between Swedish bankers and various politicians on several key projects.

There was talk that sometime in the next five years,

her parents might return home so her mother could run for senate in Virginia. "Then I'll take over the social calendar," her father had quipped more than once during their last visit that summer.

The ride home was quiet. Hannah wondered if Buddy was praying. Buddy was a man who talked to God, and most nights he'd tell her he was praying for her—something she didn't quite understand. God—if there was a God—seemed far away and uninvolved. Hannah wasn't sure if He had time to know who the real Hannah Roberts was, the reason she ran from one event to another without ever taking a day off.

"Things okay at school?" Buddy took a slow left turn onto the hilly road that led to The Colony.

"Great." Hannah yawned. "Aced my speech on the challenges of international politics, tore up in cheerleading, and designed the layouts for a third of the yearbook."

"You mean you didn't solve world hunger between classes?" Buddy's voice was upbeat, teasing her.

"Not today." She pressed her head back into the leather seat. "Maybe tomorrow."

"You'll probably try." Buddy chuckled. "Busy, busy girl. You sound like a twenty-five-year-old grad student. Not a high school freshman."

"My teachers say that." She breathed out. This was her resting time, and she made the most of it. She could've fallen asleep in the backseat of the new Lincoln.

"I guess it comes from hanging out with adults. That and staying busy."

"But you're a kid first, Miss Hannah. Don't forget that."

"I'm all right, Buddy. Staying busy keeps me sane." Her feet were sore, and she wiggled her toes as she stretched them out in front of her. That was the nice thing about Town Cars. Lots of leg room. "I have to be moving."

"That's because you're a butterfly, Miss Hannah. Nothing could ground you."

Hannah smiled. She liked that. A butterfly. Dear, sweet Buddy Bingo. He was a single man, the age of a grandfather. Blue eyes with a shock of white hair on his head and his face. Her friends thought he looked like Santa Claus, and when Hannah was little she used to wonder herself. He'd been a faithful driver for the Roberts family since Hannah was in third grade.

They pulled into the spacious entrance to The Colony and stopped at the guard station. Buddy waved to the man in the booth, and the man raised the gate. Buddy was beyond passwords at this point; all the guards knew him. When they pulled up at her house, he stopped the car and turned around, the way he always did. "How can I pray for you, Miss Hannah?"

Buddy asked her this every time he drove her. Usually she shrugged and told him it didn't matter; he could pray however he liked. But this time she thought a little longer.

"I know: pray for a miracle." She could feel her expression warm at the idea. "A Christmas miracle."

"Okay." Buddy gave a thoughtful nod of his head. "But Christmas miracles are the biggest, most amazing ones of all." He squinted. "Any certain kind of Christmas miracle?"

"I'm not sure yet." She grabbed her bags and waited for Buddy to open her door. One of her friends had talked about Christmas miracles during the yearbook meeting. The idea sounded good. Christmas miracles. Whatever that meant. And since Buddy was willing to pray, she might as well ask.

He got out, walked to her door, and opened it. "Well, Miss Hannah, you let me know if you decide. Meanwhile, I'll pray just like you asked. For a Christmas miracle."

It was a nice thought, one that settled her racing spirit and gave her peace even as her dance instructor forced ten minutes of pirouettes at the end of practice that evening.

She didn't see her grandmother until ten o'clock as she trudged up to her suite. "Hannah." The elderly woman stood, proud and stiff, outside the double doors of her own bedchamber. "How was your day?"

"Very well, Grandmother." It was always *Grandmother.* She stopped three steps short of the landing. "Thank you for asking."

"Have you brought up the B in Spanish?"

It was Hannah's only low mark. She bit the inside of her cheek. "Yes, Grandmother. It's an A-minus now."

"Very well." The woman smiled, and in it was a hint of warmth. "You'll have it up to a solid A soon, I imagine."

"Yes." Hannah took another step. "Soon."

"I assume you finished your work in class today?" Her grandmother raised her chin. "It's very late for extra attention to your studies at this hour."

"I'm finished, thank you." Hannah looked at her grandmother and felt the corners of her lips push up into her cheeks. The woman was too formal, too taken with her parents' world, their money. But still, she was all Hannah had, the only family she shared her daily life with.

The conversation stalled, and her grandmother bid her goodnight.

Not until Hannah was alone in her room did she let the truth she'd found out earlier today set in—a truth she couldn't share with anyone yet, not even Buddy Bingo.

Her parents wouldn't be coming home for Christmas this year.

They'd sent her an e-mail that morning before school. Usually they visited in summer and at Christmas—both times for a few weeks. But this year the schedule at the embassy was too busy.

"The social calendar is full, my dear," her mother wrote. "I'm afraid we'll be Christmas'ing in Sweden this year."

And like that, Hannah's Christmas had gone down the drain. Without her parents, there would be no Christmas parties or trips into the city to see the Living Christmas Tree and the annual pageant performances in the theater district. No one to exchange presents with or share a cup of cocoa with on Christmas Eve.

Her parents were even busier than she was, so she wouldn't miss out on any deep conversation or sentimentality or warm, cozy traditions—the things that made up Millie's and Kathryn's Christmas holidays. But without her parents home, the time would be quiet and lonely, just her and her grandmother—a woman who didn't believe in wasting resources every twenty-fifth of December simply because the calendar read, "Christmas."

She pulled off her dance clothes, tossed them into the hamper, and laid her blazer and skirt on the back of the sofa. The housekeepers preferred she didn't hang up her own clothing. Their method was better, easier to work with.

When the lights were off she lay there, considering her friend Kathryn's comment from earlier in the day again. *"I just wish I knew what you were running from."*

The idea bounced around her brain like a pinball. She was running from a dozen things, wasn't she? From her empty mansion and her grandmother's unsmiling face, from quiet dinners and a forgotten childhood. And now she was running from Christmas. At least when her parents came home for the holidays she could convince herself they cared. They might not talk to her much or show a genuine interest in her life the way other parents did, but at least they came.

Now, though, there was no denying the obvious. Her parents had chosen their friends and social obligations over spending Christmas with their daughter. She felt a stinging in the corners of her eyes.

Of course she was running.

Every time she thought about the e-mail a sad sort of ache started in her belly. An ache that hurt all the way to her heart. If she didn't keep busy, running from one obligation to another, the hurt would eat her alive. It shouted at her now, reminding her that no one really cared, no one knew the private places in her heart.

They especially didn't know about the memories.

Now, in the dark, they came to her again. Memories that crept through the window and kept her company on cold November nights like this one. She remembered herself as a little girl, three or four years old, sitting in a small living room—a space no bigger than her walk-in closet. She was looking at her mother—a much younger version of her mother—and in the memory she was sitting near the feet of a handsome, strapping man, and the man was playing a guitar.

The song ended and the man pulled her into his arms. He nuzzled his face against hers and the two of them rubbed noses and she felt like the luckiest little girl in the world. In the memory, her daddy loved her. Both her parents did. There were other memories, all from about the same time, and in each one her parents were happy and laughing. Talking to her and holding her and reading to her and getting down on the floor to play with her.

She opened her eyes and stared at the ceiling ten feet overhead. In the darkness she could barely make out the molding along the perimeter of the room. Here was the problem: if that was the memory, where had it come from? And why had her parents changed?

Even when they did come home, they were busy entertaining dignitaries stateside, busy throwing parties for political friends they hadn't seen since their last visit. Almost none of their time was set aside for her. The family chauffeur cared more about her life.

She thought of Buddy Bingo and the notion of a Christmas miracle and a chill ran down her arms. She knew what she wanted now, what he could pray for. She would tell him the details tomorrow; that way, if he was putting in an order with God in the near future he could be more specific.

What she wanted more than anything in the world would take divine help to pull off. Nothing simple like a new handbag or a trip to France. What she wanted was bigger than that: she wanted her parents to come home for Christmas. When she'd received the e-mail that morning, Hannah had written back. "How completely understandable that my parents would choose parties in Sweden over Christmas with me. Love you, too."

Her mother's response was quick and to the point.

"It's impossible this year, Hannah. We'll see you during summer vacation."

And that was that. In fact, at this point—with her mother's social calendar booked through the holidays and her father entertaining princes at the embassy—it would take more than wishful thinking to get her parents home.

It would take a miracle.

A Christmas miracle.

CHAPTER ONE

*M*otherhood never slowed Carol Roberts. Not when she'd first had Hannah fifteen years ago, and not now.

Back when Hannah was born, her father took care of her. He was smitten by the dark-haired, blue-eyed baby from the moment she came home. Hannah was a good girl. When she was old enough for kindergarten she was easily top of the class, and she held that distinction up until her current year as freshman at Thomas Jefferson College Preparatory. Carol was proud of her. But Hannah was still a child, and ambitious career plans didn't mix with children. Even the nicest children.

That's why Carol didn't mind living half a world away from Hannah. The two kept in touch through e-mail and phone calls, and twice a year—summer and Christmas—Carol and her husband found their way back to the States for a visit. Hannah wouldn't have had any normal sort of life living overseas, and it wasn't as if they had any choice.

Carol's husband was ambassador to Sweden.

The role of ambassador came with a host of responsibilities—some political, some practical, and some purely social in the name of goodwill. That November numerous dignitaries had passed through the office, and plans had been made for a round of holiday parties that would involve key international politicians—all of whom deserved the attention of Jack Nelson Roberts Jr.

Carol loved being in the middle of it all. Whether the day's work included a luncheon with visiting influentials or a party at a nearby ballroom, she thrived in her husband's arena, being a part of what he did—not only to help him look good, but because she had political aspirations of her own.

Maybe when Jack was finished with his work at the Swedish embassy, they could return to Maryland and she could try her hand at an office—something small to start with—and eventually work her way to being a representative, or a senator, even. She would be closer to Hannah that way. By then her daughter would be older—old enough that Carol could hire her as an intern and the two could get to know each other better.

For now, though, that type of day-in, day-out relationship would have to wait. Life at the embassy was simply too busy, too important, to take a chance on missing a key party or business dinner. Never had there been so many people to connect with, so valuable a host of politicians to get acquainted with. They were doing the United States a favor by giving the job their complete attention as winter approached. That was the reason they'd made their decision about the holidays.

This Christmas—for the first time—there would be no trip home. The holiday social demands on the embassy were too great to leave behind. Late the night before, Carol had alerted Hannah about the conflict. There would be a change of plans, she told her daughter. "Your father and I won't be coming home for Christmas after all," she wrote. "Not this year."

She'd hoped Hannah would understand. Christmas was just another day, after all. Another day in a round of parties and celebrating and merriment that went from September to January, and January to June, one year into the next for the Roberts family. Certainly Hannah could get through one Christmas without being dragged to a round of adult parties in Washington, D.C. In fact, Carol had expected Hannah might be relieved. The revised plan meant Hannah could spend the holidays relaxing with her grandmother or visiting her school friends.

But Hannah's response had been short, almost jaded.

"Fine, Mother," she'd shot back in an e-mail that morning. "How completely understandable that my parents would choose parties in Sweden over Christmas with me. Love you, too."

Love you, too? Carol had stared at those words, puzzled.

What sort of response was that? The letter made Carol wonder if she'd made a gargantuan mistake with Hannah all these years, if she'd grossly underestimated Hannah's acceptance of her lifestyle.

Ever since returning to the D.C. area, Carol had assumed her daughter understood her position. The Roberts family wasn't like regular families. There was a price to pay for Jack's title, both when he was a senator, and now as an ambassador. It wasn't so unusual, really. Nearly all of Hannah's school friends had parents whose lives involved political obligations. Senators stationed in Washington, D.C., spent half their time with their constituents in offices across the country. And those involved with international politics spent most of the year overseas.

It was a way of life.

So why the attitude from Hannah? As if Christmas wouldn't be the same if she and Jack didn't come? Carol fixed herself a salad for lunch and mulled over the situation. Hannah was beyond the sentimentality of the working class, wasn't she? The girl understood their lifestyle, how power and position came with a certain type of independence, one that didn't have room for hurt feelings or needy pairings between parents and children.

She loved Hannah, of course—loved her the way mothers in her social strata best loved their children. Not with gushy hugs or kisses or flowery words, but with actions. The proper way. Carol and Jack paid for the house in The Colony and tuition at TJ Prep, the best education a child could ask for. Beyond that they provided Hannah private instruction in dance, voice, and piano, and finishing school. In a few short years, Carol had plans for her daughter to work with her.

That was love, wasn't it?

But as Carol finished her salad, as she made her way to the back door and studied the meticulous gardens around the cobblestone patio, she thought of something she hadn't before: maybe Hannah was lonely. She was still young, after all. Maybe her schoolwork and lessons and practices had worn her out, and left her wanting adult company more than a quiet grandmother could give.

The clock ticked out a steady rhythm in the background and a pleasant lemony smell wafted through the kitchen, the result of something the housekeeper was working on in the next room. Carol squinted at the sunsprayed shrubs in the back of the yard. Yes, that had to be the problem. Hannah simply wanted a little life in the old house.

So who could spend Christmas with Hannah? She and Jack were out of the question, at least for now. But there had to be someone in their circle, someone besides Grandmother Paul, who could spend a few days with Hannah over the Christmas break.

Then, for the first time in years, a thought came to Carol.

Maybe it was time to tell her about Mike Conner. Mike, who had been Carol's first love, the man she lived with for nearly four years after Hannah was born. The man Hannah knew nothing about.

Her biological father.

Carol had hoped to wait until Hannah was eighteen to tell her, but she was fifteen now. That was old enough, wasn't it? She held her breath as she made her way through the kitchen and into her office. The box was still tucked away under the desk, in the corner of the room. The box held everything that reminded Carol of her old life, the one she'd lived before she married Jack.

She remembered to exhale. Then, with quiet steps, she crossed the room, pulled the box into the middle of the floor, and removed the lid. The first thing inside was a manila envelope with a single name written in black permanent ink across the top: *Mike*.

A rush of feelings came over her and she could see the vast stretch of Pacific Ocean, hear the steady rush of waves against the shore, feel the warm sand between her toes as she sat on the beach watching him surf. She'd met him there, and from the beginning he'd had a surfboard tucked under one arm.

Carol closed her eyes and allowed the memory to have its way with her. She had been a dreamer back then, and Mike her blond, blue-eyed dream boy. Her parents had taught her about prestige and propriety and marrying well, but Carol ignored their advice. She'd been a hopeless romantic who had her own ideas about love, and all of them centered around Mike Conner.

"He's a drifter," her mother had told her. "With him you'll never amount to anything."

"He loves me, Mother," Carol insisted. "We'll find our own way."

"He's not the marrying type." Despair rang in her mother's voice. "You'll find nothing but heartbreak."

In the end, she'd been right—after four years of scrimping and barely getting by, Carol and Mike began fighting. The magic was long worn off by then, and Carol had to admit the truth in her mother's prediction. Mike wasn't the marrying type. He'd never even asked her, not until she first brought up leaving. But by then it was over. Mike had enlisted in the Army and gone to Fort Seal in Oklahoma for training. Three weeks later, alone and anxious for her old life, Carol and Hannah left one rainy April morning and never looked back.

Knowing she couldn't marry him, Carol hadn't put Mike's name on Hannah's birth certificate, and he hadn't argued about the fact. Not at first, anyway. Probably because he'd figured Carol would come around eventually, and the two of them would marry. Then he could easily add his name to Hannah's birth records.

In the months before he enlisted, he'd been anxious for it all—marriage, a proper place on Hannah's birth certificate, a family life together. But by then, Carol was ready to go home, ready for the life her parents had wanted for her. When she and Hannah said good-bye to the small beach house, Carol left behind no information or letters or forwarding address. She returned to Maryland and picked up with Jack Roberts—high-society politician and former playboy. The two were married within a year, and Carol's mother moved into Jack's guesthouse while she and Jack and Hannah took the main house—a veritable mansion.

Life improved overnight for everyone except Hannah. For two years Hannah had talked about her daddy, asking where he was and crying for him. Sometimes Jack would hold her and rock her, telling her that he was her father now. Always, though, they had known Hannah would be fine—and she was. In time she forgot about the daddy they'd left behind, believing that Jack was, indeed, her father.

But she deserved to know about Mike, and now was as good a time as any.

Carol held the envelope to her face and breathed in. It smelled old and musty and faintly like the sea, the scent of forgotten days and bygones. She opened the flap and pulled out the first picture. It was a photo of Mike and Hannah, just around the time when Hannah was starting to walk. The two were cuddled in a worn-out recliner, and Mike was reading to her. He'd always been reading to her. Hannah had one pudgy arm draped along the back of his neck, her grin reached from one ear to the other.

Carol set the picture aside and sorted through the rest of the envelope. After a few minutes she chose two photographs—the first one, and one of Mike with his surf-board, his blond hair cut short per the instructions of his Army enlisting officer. She sifted through the bag again and found a metal lapel pin—a pair of wings Mike bought in the days before he left for training.

"Daddy's gonna be a pilot one day, Hannah. An Army pilot. Then I'll have a real pair of wings." She could hear him still, full of confidence and hope that he'd make good on his dreams and give Carol the life he thought she wanted.

By the time Mike had plans to leave for training, he was worried Carol would bolt, that she'd pick up her things one day, leave with Hannah, and never look back. Before he left he'd pulled her aside and given her the wings, the ones he'd bought. Sincerity rang in his words. *"I want Hannah to have these. Make sure, okay?"*

A gust of guilt blew over Carol. She'd forgotten his request until now. Forgotten it as if he'd never even asked. She blinked and set the wings in the pile with the two photographs. At least she was taking care of it now. It wasn't too late. Besides, if Hannah were any younger she wouldn't have appreciated this—not the pictures nor the wings nor the information about Mike.

Carol sorted through the envelope and pulled out a list of details scribbled on an old, yellowed piece of note-book paper. The list represented all the information she'd had on Mike Conner back then.

She studied the sheet: his name, an old address and phone number in Pismo Beach, California. His age back then—twenty-three—and his birth date. And the fact that he'd joined the Army in early spring 1994.

That was it—all she had to remember him by.

For nearly a minute Carol studied the sheet and wondered. Was this the right thing for Hannah? The right timing? Would she be angry that she hadn't been told sooner? She hesitated and stared at the photo. It had been her decision to keep the information from Hannah. If Hannah was upset, they'd work through it, the same way they'd work through spending a Christmas apart.

Parenting wasn't much different from a business arrangement where most of the time the details ran smoothly, but some days brought disturbing news and hard work.

Carol made a copy of the detailed information and slipped it with the photos into a new envelope. Then she typed a quick letter of explanation. She was sorry about the past, but there was nothing she could do about it. Hannah needed to know. Maybe if the girl spent the holidays looking up Mike Conner, the distraction would keep her from being lonely.

Carol sealed the envelope, addressed it, and set it in the outgoing mail tray. She glanced at her watch. It was time to put together the invite list for the black-tie Christmas party.

CHAPTER   TWO

*T*he mission would be the most dangerous Mike Conner Meade had ever faced. At least that's what his commander had told him.

He dropped into a dusty canvas chair and kicked his feet up on his rumpled cot. Another week of gusty wind and blinding sand, no relief in sight. Baghdad gave new meaning to the word *desert*—even when things were cooling down. It was sky and sand, sometimes the same color, and a hot grittiness that ground itself into the spaces between his teeth and his socks and the layers of his sleeping bag. It was a parched dry heat that seemed to age him ten years in as many days.

The meeting with his commander, Colonel Jared Whalin, was set to take place in five minutes, three tents down in the shanty barracks where they lived. The meeting was private. No one knew about the mission, not yet.

If Colonel Whalin had his way, only a handful ever would.

Two minutes ticked past and then another two. Mike stretched out his legs and wondered how long it had been since he'd sat on a surfboard, his legs dangling into the ocean while he waited for the perfect wave. After three years of tours in Iraq he'd never look at sand again the same way. His surfer days felt like they belonged to another person, someone he didn't even try to remember.

He checked his watch. It was time.

He stood, shook his pants legs down around his boots, pressed his lips together, and slipped out through the flap in his tent. A burst of wind and sand hit him in the face and he squinted hard. Every step felt like a countdown to destiny—a destiny he had avoided every year, every mission, until now. He breathed in through his nose. Days like this he wished he hadn't given up smoking.

"Meade, that you?"

Meade. That was the name they knew him by—his legal last name. Conner, his middle name and the name he'd actually used all his civilian life, wasn't something that had followed him into the Army. Mike Meade. That was who he was now. No surfer-boy nicknames for the U.S. military.

Mike grabbed the canvas flap and stepped inside. "Yes, sir." He straightened and gave a sharp salute. He had to talk over the sound of the wind and the flapping tent. "You wanted to talk about the mission, sir?"

"Yes." Colonel Whalin sat behind his desk, one elbow anchored amid a slew of documents. He gestured in Mike's direction. "At ease." He sounded tired, defeated. "Listen, Meade, we don't want you to run this mission. Assign it to someone else."

Mike spread his legs apart and allowed his spine and shoulders to relax. He had expected this. "Can you run through the details, sir? I'm a little unclear."

The colonel sorted through the paperwork in front of him. "One of these days we'll pack up our tents and go home, you know that?" He rested his forearms on the desk. "But we're not quite there, not yet."

"Sir." Mike wouldn't say more. Not until the man got more specific.

A long sigh passed through the colonel's gray teeth. "We found the headquarters for a group of insurgents just outside Baghdad, you know that much, right?"

"Yes, sir."

"Well," the colonel narrowed his eyes. "They're set up in an old, abandoned grade school." He waved his hand in the air, disgusted. "Living quarters, training compound, the whole works. Hiding where kids used to play."

"The goal, sir?"

The colonel leveled his gaze at Mike. "The mission is two-fold." He pulled a pack of Camels from his pocket, tapped it twice, and slipped a cigarette between his lips. "Fly six Rangers in at night, rappel onto the roof of the building adjacent to their dorm area. The

Rangers break in through the windows, capture the insurgents, and get back out. A ground crew will be waiting to pick up the men. But you'll provide air cover. We're looking at ten, eleven minutes tops."

Mike swallowed. *Eleven minutes?* The chopper would be the biggest target in the area, stationary long enough for an insurgent to grab a rocket-propelled grenade and bring the bird down three times over. No wonder Colonel Whalin had told him it was dangerous. He looked straight ahead. "The second part?"

"Reconnaissance." He pulled a lighter from the top drawer of his desk and lit his cigarette. "We have a feeling they're holding prisoners there. You and your copilot will have night-vision goggles, of course. We want as much information as you can get."

"Will we use a gunner, sir?" Not all missions included a gunner at the open door of the chopper. But if the chopper was going to hang in the air for eleven minutes, it would be a must.

"Definitely." The colonel rubbed his eyes. His throat was thick. "There'll be nine men altogether. Pilot, copilot, the gunner, and six Rangers." He took a long drag from his cigarette. "A lot rides on it, Meade. We need someone capable. But let's use the young guys. A dispensable crew."

"Beg your pardon, sir." Mike clenched his jaw. "I don't have a crew like that."

"I know." Colonel Whalin pinned the cigarette between his lips and tossed up his hands. His tone was gravelly. "You get what I mean. The mission's dangerous. It's crazy dangerous."

Mike unclenched his jaw. "I figured it was something like that, sir. I'm not worried; I can handle it."

"Of course you can handle it." His commander let the cigarette dangle from his lower lip. "Your crew's the best we've got, Meade. I want you to think about the other crews, all five of them." He inhaled sharply and let the smoke filter out through his nose. "I need an answer by tomorrow. Your top two choices."

"Sir, what if I want to go?" Mike didn't flinch. It wasn't a matter of hiding his fear. He simply had none. His copilot was single, a guy everyone called CJ. The two of them were legend in wartime missions. Legend getting in and out of situations like the one the colonel had just described.

They would handle the mission better than anyone.

"At this point, we want someone else. You and Ceej are my ace crew. The best we've got." Colonel Whalin pinched his cigarette between his second and third fingers and brought it down to desk level. "Give it some thought. We want the insurgents gone before the next Iraqi election."

"January, sir?"

"Yes. January." The colonel checked a document on his desk. Outside the wind howled against the tent. "December 12." His tone was flat. "That's D-Day." He took another drag and held it. After a few seconds he brushed his hand out in front of him. The smoke curled up from his lips. "Get back to your quarters. We'll talk tomorrow."

"Thank you, sir."

The colonel dismissed him, and two minutes later Mike was back in his tent, sitting on the edge of his cot. He linked his fingers at the base of his neck and stared at his boots.

Someone dispensable?

He went down the list. Joe and Sage and Larry and Gumbo were the two crews with the least experience, and eleven children between them. Tito and Fossie were fresh off their honeymoons. Andy and Stoker, and Jimbo and Junior all had kids on the way. He worked his fingers into the muscles at the base of his neck and turned his head first one way, then the other.

All five of the other crews were made up of men with a reason to live.

But what about him and CJ? No wives, no family. Nothing to lose. It was part of what made the two of them such good chopper pilots. They took risks other pilots wouldn't, but they always came out on top. No fear, no failure. Wasn't that what they told each other?

The fact that he and Ceej had more experience didn't make them less dispensable. It made them more likely to come out alive. If anyone could handle the mission, they could. With CJ by his side, he could hover a chopper twenty minutes if he had to. They would spot an insurgent with an RPG and duck out for a few minutes if they had to. They could have the gunner fire on anyone aiming anything in their direction. Never mind the odds; they could handle the mission better than any of the crews. With CJ, Mike could take the cockpit and fly with nerves of steel, no reservations, nothing in his rearview mirror.

He reached under his cot and felt the worn brown paper sack.

Nothing but this.

CHAPTER THREE

*M*ike scanned the rest of the cots in his tent—the men spread out, snoring beneath their dusty sheets. A single light hung above him, bright enough to see the contents of the bag if he wanted to. And tonight he did. He slid it out and stared at it. It wasn't much, the bag. Just a little bigger than an average lunch sack. The top was scrunched closed and worn around the edges, proof that Mike had carried it with him for eleven years. Wherever his cot was set up, the bag was beneath it.

He opened the mouth of the bag, and with careful hands he took out the contents. He spread them on his sheet and looked at the items one at a time. There was a photo of Hannah in his arms when she was an infant, and another taken three years later that showed the two of them building a sandcastle on the beach. Scattered among the items were the broken clay pieces of a miniature playhouse she'd made for him with modeling clay she'd gotten for her third birthday.

"You and me, Daddy." Her little girl singsong voice sounded in his heart every time he saw the broken pieces. *"This'll be our house someday."*

Funny how even back then she hadn't mentioned her mother. Daddy and me this, and daddy and me that. Hannah had liked her mother, but Carol had been more of a kindhearted roommate than a caring, involved parent.

"She needs you," Mike could hear himself telling Carol. "Spend a little time with her, why don't you?"

"I already told you." Carol would toss her brown hair and scowl at him. "I wasn't ready to be a mother. That sort of thing doesn't just happen when the baby comes. It takes time."

Lots of things didn't happen when the baby came. He had convinced her to have Hannah in the first place, and once that part was decided, he'd done his best to make them both happy. Three years later, when she hinted at leaving, he brought home a wedding ring and asked her to be his wife. But by then she had school and careers on her mind. "We can get married later," she told him.

Mike moved his fingers over the broken clay pieces from the bag. His eyes fell on something else—a folded piece of lined paper. The creases were yellowed from age; a few of them had worn through the page, leaving long, narrow slits in the paper. He opened it and felt himself smile, the way he always smiled when he looked at the crayoned drawing.

Hannah had made it for him two weeks before he left for basic training. It was a little girl consisting of a big head, short stick legs, and round blue eyes. Stick arms stuck out straight on either side, and one appeared to be attached to an equally straight stick arm belonging to a man. Both of them had oversized U-shaped smiles, and a not-quite-round yellow sun took up the left side of the sky above them. On the right side she had written her first sentence: *Hannah loves Daddy.*

That was it—all he had to remember her by, all he had to push him on the days when he thought he'd never leave the desert alive. Whenever he felt himself getting down, he checked the bag. The clay pieces and photographs, the folded drawing, were enough to remind him of the most important thing:

He had to come home alive so he could find her.

Back when they all lived together in his father's house a block from the beach, Mike had felt things falling apart. Carol came from money. At first she found Mike and his simple existence refreshing and daring, but eventually the novelty wore off. By the time Hannah was two, Carol complained about their living conditions.

"Lifeguards are drifters, Mike." She would put her hands on her hips. "I love you, but I need more than this. There must be something else you can do."

He hadn't known what, but one day he heard two of

the other guards talking about the Air Force. Four years. Free education and career training. Maybe something like that would make Carol happy. He went with his buddies to the recruiting office and smiled big at the man behind the desk.

"I want to be a pilot, sir. Is this the right place?"

The man sized him up. "You got a four-year degree, son?"

Mike felt his shoulders slump a little. "No, sir. I figured I'd get that in the Air Force—while I was learning how to fly planes."

"Right." The man smiled. "It doesn't work that way in the Air Force, son. But I tell you what. You go next door and go through a door marked 'Army,' and you can sign up to be a chopper pilot." He smiled again. "How's that sound?"

A chopper pilot? Mike took only a few seconds to mull over the idea. Flying choppers wouldn't be bad. He remembered a comment Carol had made—that she'd always figured she'd marry a politician or an officer, someone of stature. He cleared his throat. "Could I be an officer if I flew choppers in the Army?"

"Definitely." The man gave a firm nod. He pointed to the door. "You learn how to fly a chopper and you'll be an Army warrant officer, son."

Doubt flashed in his mind. "How long, sir? How long for training?" Carol would only be patient so long.

"Eight weeks for basic," the man stroked his chin.

"Maybe another eight to twelve weeks for tech training. Then you'd be off to a base where you'd spend the next eighteen months learning to fly choppers."

Eight weeks of basic and another eight plus weeks of tech training? Mike did the math in his head. That meant at least four months away from Carol and Hannah. But after that they could be together on the base while he went to pilot school. A surge of ambition welled up within him. The plan was all he had, the only way he could become the sort of man Carol wanted him to be.

He nodded at the man behind the desk. "Thank you, sir." He gave a quick salute and a smile. "I'll be heading next door now."

In a matter of hours he was no longer a carefree surfer, a lifeguard at the beach. He was an Army man, a person with a potential and a future. When Carol came home from school that night, Mike was ready with the news. He grinned at her and held up the Army folder. "I figured everything out," he told her. "Wait'll you hear."

Carol waited, but she had one foot out the door almost before he was finished with the details. "Army? Mike, are you crazy?" She huffed and tossed her designer bag on the scuffed tabletop. "I don't want to marry an Army man! I wanna be the wife of a lawyer or a professor or a politician. Something . . ." She waved her hands about in front of her face, frustrated. "Something with a little class and prestige."

"I'll be an officer, Carol. That has to count for something."

"An Army officer, Mike? Are you serious?"

Her words were like bullets, ripping holes in the fragile plans he'd laid out for himself. Training would take him away for sixteen weeks, but it took only days to figure out Carol's course of action.

"I need time, Mike. I need to be with my parents."

"It's not like I'm leaving you, Carol." He clenched his jaw. "I'll be gone four months, that's all."

"So maybe I spend that time back at home, and then we can talk."

"Talk, Carol?"

"Yes." Her voice was frantic, anxious. She exhaled and made an obvious attempt to calm herself. "Talk about whether we'll still have a reason to be together."

Mike could tell by looking at her that she was going to leave. There was nothing he could do to stop her. "What about Hannah?"

"You can see her. With or without me." Carol touched his shoulder, her eyes more tender than before. "Get through training and then you can look us up."

Mike should've known better, should've realized the dangerous situation he was in when it came to Hannah. But even in his most uncharitable moments, he never once imagined that Carol would leave with his daughter, disappear without a trace or a trail. It never occurred to him that he would spend the next eleven years searching for the dark-haired little girl who had worked her way into the fabric of his soul.

He started his training and convinced himself Carol would move to the base, that she'd marry him and they could live together while he was in pilot training. Surely she would realize his potential and jump at the chance for the three of them to be a family again. They talked three times in the early weeks before she and Hannah left for her parents' house.

"I'll go for a month, that's all. Don't call me, Mike. I'll call you." Carol told him before she moved. "My parents need time to adjust."

Carol called him once from her parents' house. At the end of the call she put Hannah on the line.

"Hi, Daddy."

"Hi, sugar." Mike's heart beat so hard he expected it to burst through his chest and bounce around on the floor. "I miss you."

"Miss you, too." Her singsong voice sounded sad, flat. "Come home, Daddy. Mommy doesn't read to me."

"Where is home, baby?" Mike wasn't testing her. He only wondered what Carol had told her.

"I'm with Grandmother and Grandfather." Hannah thought for a moment. "But home is where you are, Daddy. So come, okay?"

Mike could barely speak by the time Hannah handed the phone back to Carol. After that the phone calls stopped. When he finished training, the only information he had for her wound up being a bad address and a wrong phone number.

At first Mike drove himself crazy looking for her.

He checked phonebooks and called schools and churches in the Virginia and Washington, D.C., area, desperate to find her. He was sure he'd find them in a matter of weeks. His little Hannah needed him, and Carol had promised. She wouldn't keep him from her.

But the weeks slipped into months as his training continued. Every chance he had he looked for them, and even when five years became seven and then nine he held out hope. She was out there somewhere. Carol had married, of course. That was the reason he couldn't find anyone by her last name. But still they were somewhere.

It wasn't until his recent deployment, the past year in the desert that his hope began to erode. She would be fifteen now, far too old to remember him even if he could find her. If he survived Iraq, it was time to move on, to find another life. Time to let go of the one he'd imagined in his heart and mind every time he climbed into a fighter jet.

He looked at the scattered remains of the dream, the broken pottery and aging artifacts. One at a time he placed them back in the bag and crumpled the neck closed again. He would always keep the bag, but only as a reminder of what used to be. His fingers tightened around the bag and he held his breath.

It was over. The hoping and searching and believing

that he'd find his Hannah again . . . all of it was over. It had been over a lot longer than he cared to admit. No wonder he could look his commander in the face and tell him the truth straight up. The mission belonged to him. He was perfect for the job. Not so much because of his experience, but because of his lack of connection. He had no family, no wife, no dark-haired daughter to come home to. No one to grieve his loss if he never made it out alive. CJ was no different.

He clenched his jaw and slid the bag back beneath his bed. His commander was right. Maybe some men were dispensable.

And if that were true, maybe he was one of them.

CHAPTER FOUR

*T*he house was dark like always.

Hannah stepped out of the Town Car, waved good-bye to Buddy Bingo, and crept through the front door. The lights were off, same as outside. A chill ran down Hannah's arms, a combination of the quiet darkness and a draft that always marked the entryway of their home.

"Grandmother?"

There was no answer, and Hannah frowned. Sometimes she went days without seeing her grandmother, since the older woman went to bed early and woke up late. It was more like living alone all the time. She sighed and the sound rattled in the foyer. She closed the door behind her and dropped her gym bag. Cheerleading had been brutal and she had only half an hour until dance.

A light switch near the door lit up much of the downstairs. Hannah walked past the marble fountain that separated the entrance from the formal living room. She was about to head up to her bedroom when something on the dining room table caught her attention. She stopped and peeked around the corner. It was a package of some kind, a manila envelope.

Strange. Hannah walked closer, curious. Her grandmother took care of the mail, so what was this? She peered at it. *Miss Hannah Roberts,* it read. She opened her mouth and a soft gasp came out. The package was from her mother. After days of silence, not even an e-mail, her mother had sent her something.

She tore open the package and spread the contents on the table. A bulky white envelope, and next to it a single sheet of note paper and a hand-written letter. Hannah picked it up. Her mother's handwriting was familiar, but only vaguely so. She rarely sent packages from Sweden. Hannah let her eyes find the top of the note.

Dear Hannah,

You might not understand what I'm about to tell you, but I think it's time. I wanted to wait until you were eighteen, old enough to check into this information and make some decisions for yourself. Having Christmas all alone, you'll have time to think this through.

This is it: Jack isn't your biological father.

Hannah's knees trembled and she grabbed hold of the back of the closest chair. *What?* She moved her eyes over the line again, but the words wouldn't come together, wouldn't form into a logical sentence. Her mother must be crazy, sending her a note like this. She tried again and this time the words slammed at her like a series of rough waves, each one knocking a little more wind from her.

Jack Roberts isn't my biological father? A sharp stinging started in the corners of her eyes. This couldn't be right. Of course Jack was her father. Her parents wouldn't have lied about that all these years . . . would they? She swallowed hard, pulled out the chair, and sat down. Her vision was blurred, and she blinked, finding her place on the note.

Your father's name is Mike Conner. I've enclosed some details about him, but I know very little. I haven't spoken to him since we parted. But what information I do have is on a sheet of paper in the envelope, also.

Hannah took three quick breaths and gave a sharp shake of her head. This wasn't happening, it couldn't be. She'd never heard the name *Mike Conner* before, so how could it be true? How could he be her father? Her heart thumped hard within her, a little more convinced than her mind and soul. Her mother wasn't a liar; though she wanted to rip up the letter, throw it in the trash, and pretend she'd never opened the package, that single truth kept her reading.

Hannah, there was a time when I loved Mike very much. But he wasn't the sort of man I could marry; I hope you understand, darling. We were together until your fourth birthday and then our lives took us in different directions. There are more details, information I'll share with you some day when we're together. For now, this is all you need to know. Inside the envelope are some photographs and a pair of wings he bought before he joined the Army. It was something Mike wanted you to have.

I suppose I should've told you this face to face. But for some reason I felt this was the time. Don't hold it against me, Hannah. Jack will always consider you his daughter, and he will be no less a father to you simply because you know the truth. Instead try to be adult about it. I know you will be. You're a good girl. Talk to you soon,
Mother

Hannah stared at the page. The only sounds were her heartbeat and the rustling of the note, still clutched in her trembling hand. She couldn't take it all in, couldn't rationalize about whether the information was or wasn't true. But her mother obviously thought it was true, and that meant . . .

She set the note down and reached for the stuffed white envelope. Carefully, as if it contained something too terrifying, too sacred, to examine, she slid her finger under the flap and slit open the top. Her heartbeat was louder than the envelope shaking in her hands. Her mind screamed at her, willing her to put it down. But she continued, moving slowly, trancelike.

The first thing she pulled from it was a photograph.

Hannah's breathing wasn't right, and she couldn't blink as she stared at the image in the picture. It was her—a little-girl version of herself—cuddled on the lap of a handsome blond man. The man was reading to her.

Again Hannah's mouth fell open. Gradually, like the changing colors in fall, the picture of her past began to come into focus. If the little girl was her—and she knew it was because of other baby pictures she'd seen—then the blond man would be Mike Conner. And if he was Mike . . .

A series of dots inside her mind connected at lightning speed. The lines in her memory came into crisp focus. If he was her father, and he liked to read to her, then maybe Mike Conner was the man in her memories. The one who sang with his guitar and got down on the floor to play with her.

Her hands shook harder, and she worked to steady the image. Something about his eyes looked familiar, and after a minute she figured it out. His eyes were the same ones she looked at in the mirror every day. Hers couldn't have been more like his—the shape, the color. Even the arch of her eyebrows.

The tears were back, spilling from the confused corners of her soul straight into her eyes, clouding her vision again and making her wonder at the feelings coming over her. Anger at her mother, of course. Because how could she lie about something so important? And for so many years? And maybe more anger because if her memories—the good memories—were about Mike Conner, then . . . how could her mother have left him?

But there were other feelings, too. So many others.

Confusion because this new truth still felt like a joke or a trick. Fear because her world was tumbling off center, wobbling and falling and threatening to break into a million tiny pieces. And curiosity because if it really was true, then she wanted to meet him. As soon as possible, so she could ask him if he was the one. The daddy in her dreams.

And over all of it was sadness. Because it had to be true; the picture in her hand told her so. Only now she was almost grown up and she'd lost ten years, a decade, with the man in the picture. Sadness because maybe he'd forgotten about her the way she had forgotten about him.

She laid the photograph down carefully on the table in front of her. Then she reached back into the envelope and pulled out another one. This picture was of the same man standing on the beach in shorts and a T-shirt. A surfboard was tucked under his arm.

Her mother's voice came to mind, faded by the years: *"Don't go near the water, Hannah. Stay here on the towel with Daddy."*

That was it. Nothing more came to mind. But her

mother's warning was as real as if she were standing up-stairs shouting down at her. It was another clue, further proof that the photographs weren't a figment of her imagination. When she was little, her mother had warned her about the water—the ocean, probably. And Mike Conner was a surfer.

Another few dots connected.

The next item in the envelope was a sheet with Mike's name and birth date and the fact that he'd lived in Pismo Beach. A few other bits of information. And last inside was the lapel pin, the wings her mother had mentioned in the note. Hannah ran her thumb gently over the metal surface and held it up, noting the gray-and-black detail. Had he become a pilot, then? Someone flying for the Army?

A knock sounded at the door and she jumped. Her dance teacher! She set the pin and the photos back in the envelope and put the envelope back inside the bigger manila packaging. Whatever truth lay in her mother's note, she'd have to sort through it later.

Hannah let her dance teacher in and apologized for not being ready. Then she raced to her room, threw on her tights and leotard, and met the teacher in the dance room downstairs. For the next hour she practiced pirou-ettes and jazz leaps, but all the while she barely heard the music or the teacher chiding her to land lighter or jump higher.

Jack wasn't her father?

The blond man in the pictures overtook every other thought until finally the lesson was over and she scurried the manila package to her room. There she read her mother's note again and pulled out the photos from the envelope. Before she fell asleep that night she stared at the photos for a long time. That's when she realized another feeling had been added to the mix.

Happiness.

Because maybe it wasn't too late. Maybe, if Mike Conner was the daddy in her memories, she could find him again and they could start up loving each other where they left off all those years ago. Maybe the blond man would be her father, and Jack would be nothing more than a nice man who had married her mother.

Which was all he'd ever been, anyway.

She fell asleep and this time the memories of her long-ago daddy sprang to life in her dreams. In them she was chasing him down a sandy beach, giggling like mad when he turned around and caught her up over his shoulder.

The next morning she dressed in her favorite jeans and denim jacket, and on the lapel she pinned the wings. The wings Mike Conner had told her mother to give her.

Normally she didn't wake her grandmother before going to school, but this was an emergency. She would know if her mother's note was right, or if the information about Mike Conner was some sort of trick or mistake.

She was completely ready for school when she gave a light knock on the door into her grandmother's suite. "Hello?"

For a moment, there was only silence. Then she heard movement from behind the door. "Hannah? Is that you?"

"Yes. Can we speak for a minute, please?"

Her grandmother opened the door, a slight scowl creasing her forehead. "*May* we speak for a minute, you mean."

Hannah exhaled quietly. Propriety always came before purpose. That was her grandmother's rule, no matter what the situation. "May we speak for a minute, please?"

"Certainly." Her grandmother wore her long blue-velvet robe, the one she'd had for the past year. She stepped aside, and the robe swished around her ankles. "Come in."

"Thank you." Hannah hated this—the formality. But it was all they'd ever known. She followed her grandmother into the spacious room. The words were on her tongue, rehearsed. But before she could speak them, her grandmother's scowl deepened and her eyes grew wide. She was looking at the wings.

"What—" She pointed to the pin. "—is that?"

Hannah blinked. "Well, Grandmother. That's what I'd like to talk to you about."

Her grandmother's face looked paler than before,

almost as white as her linen bedspread. "They're pilot wings."

"Yes." Hannah gulped. Without realizing it, she fingered the pin. "My mother sent them."

"She . . ." Her grandmother's eyes lifted. "Did she say why she'd do such a thing?"

Hannah twisted her fingers together and shifted from one foot to the other. "Jack Roberts isn't my father, is he?"

For a long moment her grandmother stared at her, surprised. Then indignant. She took a step back. "Young lady, that's something for you and your mother."

"But he isn't, right?"

Her grandmother straightened herself and turned her back to Hannah. "Where did you hear that?"

"My mother." Hannah came closer. Her stomach twisted. "She sent me the wings and two photos and a note."

Her grandmother whirled around. "Photos?"

Hannah hesitated. "Pictures of Mike Conner." Her mouth was dry. "He's my real father, right, Grandmother?"

For a long minute her grandmother only stared at her, unmoving. Then she cleared her throat and lifted her chin. "Your mother would never lie to you, Hannah. You know that."

The thick carpet beneath her feet felt suddenly liquid. "So, it's true." Her words were breathy, a whisper, all she could force.

"Yes." Her grandmother turned toward the window again. "But I have nothing to say about him. I warned your mother not to go to California." She glanced over her shoulder at Hannah. "I taught myself to forget she ever actually did."

Hannah hugged herself. She felt faint, the way she sometimes felt when she'd gone too long without eating. Her grandmother had known about Mike all this time, and never said anything. Her entire family was in on the conspiracy. "Did you . . . did you know Mike?"

"Hannah . . ." Her grandmother spun toward her once more, and for the first time she looked less than controlled. Fear creased the skin at the corners of her eyes, and her voice was higher than before. "You need to get to school. Buddy will be waiting for you."

Anger hit Hannah then. She tightened her hands and wiggled her toes in her black dress loafers. "Grandmother, I asked you a question."

Her grandmother's voice rose another notch. "It was your mother's mistake." She pointed to the door and gave a terse nod at Hannah. "Ask her."

At first Hannah couldn't move. Two thoughts fought for position in her mind: the fact that her grandmother obviously knew something about Mike Conner, but refused to talk about him. And the possibility that maybe this was why her grandmother kept her distance—because she wasn't the child of the great Jack Roberts. Rather, she was the daughter of a California surfer.

That had to be it, the reason her grandmother had always seemed to barely tolerate her.

Hannah resisted the urge to say something spiteful to the old woman. Instead she turned around, flew down the stairs, grabbed her backpack, and ran out the front door. Tears stung at her eyes again, but she held them off. Even so, she didn't fool Buddy Bingo.

"Something wrong, Miss Hannah?" He glanced at her in the rearview mirror. "You look a little flustered."

Hannah situated herself and buckled her seat belt. She was breathing hard, keeping herself from crying. "I'm fine."

Buddy gave a slow nod and let the conversation stall until they were on the main highway to the school. Hannah's mind raced faster than her heart. How had she missed it all these years? Of course Jack Roberts wasn't her father. He never looked at her or hugged her or spent time with her the way she'd seen her friends' fathers do. The strange memories were a sign, one that had been there all along. In the soil of her heart, the truth had always lay buried, hadn't it? That the daddy in the dreams wasn't Jack Roberts, but someone else.

They were almost at school when Hannah remembered the Christmas miracle. She leaned forward and grabbed the back of Buddy's seat. "Can I ask you something?"

In the mirror, Buddy's eyes sparkled. "I've been waiting."

Hannah smiled. She should've told him the minute she climbed in. "Remember that Christmas miracle you're praying for—the one for me?"

"Sure do." He gave a firm nod of his head. "Praying every day about it."

"Good." Hannah held her breath. Fresh new possibility sat in the seat beside her. If there was a God, He wouldn't mind her being more specific, would He? She gripped the back of Buddy's seat a little more tightly. "Could you add a few more details to the prayer?"

"You bet." Buddy's smile faded. "What're the details?"

"Well . . ." She took another few deep breaths. "Pray that I can spend Christmas with my parents."

Cars whizzed on either side, and Buddy moved the Town Car over two lanes so he could turn into the school parking lot. When he was stopped, he turned and made eye contact with her. "They're not coming?"

Hannah thought about telling him the whole truth— that they weren't coming and, worse than that, Jack wasn't even her father. Instead she forced a sad smile. "No, Buddy. They're not."

He nodded, and his eyes looked watery. "Then that's what I'll pray for. That you and your parents would be together for Christmas." He paused. "But don't forget something."

"What?"

"Miracles happen to folks who believe. You gotta believe, Miss Hannah."

Believe? It was something she hadn't thought about before. "Okay. I guess I could do that." She grabbed her roller bag and patted the back of Buddy's seat. "See you later. Thanks, Buddy."

Not until she was halfway to her first class did she realize that she'd been walking with her fingers on her lapel pin, on the wings. She stopped before she reached the building and stared up at the clear blue sky.

Was he a pilot now? Had he stayed with the Army all these years? Hannah rubbed her thumb over the wings one more time.

She would wear them as long as Buddy Bingo was praying. And maybe one day she'd have more than the wings of the daddy in the memory. Maybe one day—if she believed really hard—she'd have the daddy.

The one in her dreams.

CHAPTER FIVE

*C*ongressman James McKenna had things to do. But the conversation with the girl wouldn't let him go.

He'd met her a time or two at political dinners. She was Hannah Roberts, daughter of the ambassador to Sweden, the powerful Jack Nelson Roberts Jr. And now apparently there was a family relative missing, someone the girl had only just found out about. McKenna remembered the conversation with the girl like it had just happened.

"Please, sir, my parents are busy and I can't find him by myself." She'd sounded on the verge of tears. "My mother gave me all the information she has, and . . . well, sir, it isn't enough."

Near as he could tell, the missing man—a Mike Conner—was the girl's uncle, someone she'd been very close to as a little girl. "I'll see what I can do," he told her. And now he felt stymied in every other way until he could at least point her in the right direction. It wasn't so much that she was Jack Roberts' daughter. It was the catch in her voice when she'd finished her request:

"If I can't find him, I'll spend the rest of my life looking."

McKenna sighed loud and hard. He shoved the paperwork on his desk to the side and grabbed a notebook. The details weren't much. Mike Conner from Pismo Beach, joined the Army in 1994.

He picked up the phone and called one of the top officers in the Army. He had contacts all over the country, and this was one of them. "Jennings, McKenna here. I need you to run a check on an Army man for me."

The sound of rustling paperwork came over the line. "Okay, shoot."

"Mike Conner. Joined in '94."

It took less than a minute for Jennings' answer. "We got a couple of Mike Conners. One joined in '65, and another one in 1973. Two last year. Nothing even close to '94."

"Any of them from Pismo Beach?"

"Uh . . . the one in '73 was from San Francisco. That's the closest I've got."

McKenna pinched the bridge of his nose. "You sure about the date?"

"Yes." Jennings sounded rushed. "The guy got a discharge. Hurt his leg, it looks like."

"Hmmm." McKenna doodled the name *Mike Conner* at the top of his notepad. "Okay, thanks. Maybe the information's bad." The phone call ended and McKenna tried every other branch of the service before tossing his pencil on the desk. He'd put in one more call—to a reporter contact at the *Washington Post.* Then he'd let it go. He wasn't a miracle worker, after all.

That territory belonged to Someone else altogether.

Hannah hung up the phone with the congressman and stared at the piece of notebook paper she'd ripped from her binder. The congressman had a few details, the first one enough to take her breath away. There was no sign of a Mike Conner in the Army, just a few other men with the same name, including someone who'd left with an injury.

So why couldn't the congressman find her father? He had to have been there at one time or another; her mother had been sure about that detail.

It was the congressman's last bit of information that gave her hope. Apparently he had a connection at a national country music television channel. Through the holidays they were running messages to soldiers serving in the war efforts in Iraq and Afghanistan.

Hannah might've been at the top of her class, and she might've had a better vocabulary than most adults, but even she wasn't sure what a "war effort" was. War, yes. That she understood. And if her dad was in the war, then she had no time to waste. She had to get word out that she was looking for him.

Assuming he was still in the Army.

But here was the best part of all. Even if he wasn't in the Army or anywhere overseas, he still might watch the country music channel. And if he did, then there was a chance he'd see her message.

She took a deep breath, picked up the phone, and called the channel. She wouldn't tell the man about her connection to Congressman McKenna or to Jack Roberts. No need. He was the one who took requests, and this was one request she didn't want linked to her political ties.

"Do you have a loved one in the service, miss?" The man was friendly.

Hannah felt herself relax. He wouldn't know who she was. And with all the people who watched the station's music videos, her father might just see her message. "Yes." She closed her eyes. "My dad."

"I'm sorry." He hesitated. "I'm sure you miss him a lot."

"I do."

"Well, then, what do you want to tell him?"

"You mean . . ." Hannah opened her eyes and stared out the window. It was raining, and the temperatures were colder than they'd been all winter. Snow was forecast before the end of the week. "You'll put it on the air? For sure?"

"Absolutely." There was a smile in the man's voice. "If your dad's watching, he'll see your message."

"All right, then." She'd written out what she wanted to tell him. Now she pulled that piece of paper closer and studied it. "Tell him this:

"Daddy, this is Hannah. Mom showed me the pictures, the one with you and me reading and the other one, with you and your surfboard. I'm trying to find you. So if you see this, call the station, and they'll tell you how to reach me. I love you, Daddy. I never forgot you."

She took a slow breath. "Is that good?"

The man didn't say anything at first. Then he made a coughing sound. "Honey, you mean you don't know where your daddy is?"

"No, sir." Her throat was thick. She touched the wings pinned to her sweater. "I haven't seen him since I was four. My mother said he's in the Army."

"Well, then let's get this message on the air today."

She left her phone number with the man, and he promised to get back to her if he heard anything from her father. The message she'd left was still playing in her mind when the phone rang.

Without checking Caller ID, Hannah answered it on the first ring. "Hello?"

"Hannah Roberts, please. This is Kara Dillon from the *Washington Post*."

The *Washington Post?* Hannah pulled up a bar stool and leaned hard onto the kitchen counter. "This is she."

"Okay, then . . ." The reporter hesitated, and in the background Hannah could hear voices and the tapping of computer keyboards. "Congressman McKenna told us you were trying to find a long-lost relative."

"I am." Hannah was up off her seat. This was exactly what she needed; help from the media. "I haven't seen my dad in eleven years and now I have his name and his picture but no—"

"I'm sorry." The woman didn't let her finish. "Your father? I thought your father was Jack Roberts, the politician."

Fear grabbed her around the throat and for a moment she couldn't speak. Could she do this? Could she go public with something no one else knew? In the time it took her heart to thump out a handful of beats, she remembered her mother's note. It said nothing about keeping quiet on the issue.

So what if Jack Roberts wasn't her biological father? She swallowed and forced the words in a single breath. "Jack Roberts married my mother when I was four, and he raised me as his daughter, but my real dad is Mike Conner from Pismo Beach, California, and now he's in the Army, but there's no record of him." She grabbed a quick gulp of air. "He's the one I'm looking for."

"I see." The reporter took a minute, maybe writing down this new information. "Does your . . . mother know you've gone public with your search?"

Hannah bit her lip. "Not really." What's the worst thing the paper could print? And whatever headline might run, the fallout would be worth the possibility that her dad would see it and find her. She walked out of the kitchen and dropped into a suede recliner in the den. "But I don't think she'll mind. She's the one who told me about Mike Conner."

"Well, then." The reporter sounded overly happy. "I think it'll make a perfect Christmas story. Let's go ahead with the interview."

The questions went on for nearly an hour—questions about her childhood and the memories she held of her early years with Mike Conner. Once Hannah started opening up to the woman, the answers came easily. Not until she was brushing her teeth that night, after cheer and dance and a long conversation with Kathryn about which guys might be worth going to the prom with, did she feel a hint of remorse about agreeing to the interview.

Her mother wouldn't mind, would she? Whatever the paper printed, it was bound to help her find her father, right? Besides, her mother hadn't exactly told her no. But only then, hours after the fact, did it occur to her that maybe—just maybe—she hadn't only answered the reporter's questions because of her deep need to see her dad.

But because of her need to see her mother, as well.

CHAPTER SIX

*M*ike Conner trudged through the tent to the food line, took a plate of hot chicken and gravy and a slab of bread, and found a folding chair near the television set, ten yards away. Usually he sat at one of the tables, sharing talk with the guys. But tonight he had nothing to say to anyone.

The mission was in twelve hours.

An old western played above the distant conversations—John Wayne telling somebody where to get off and why. Mike settled into his chair. The television was set up in the dining tent, as far away from the blowing sand as possible. This tent was bigger than the others, a makeshift cafeteria tucked away at the back of their temporary base. In it were a couple dozen folding chairs and rows of aluminum tables, usually filled with weary soldiers and chopper crews catching a quick meal between assignments.

Mike took a bite of the chicken and shifted it around in his mouth. Too hot, like always. After a few seconds he swallowed it and stared at the television. He rarely watched it. Life on the outside was no longer real to him, no longer something he wanted to see or be a part of.

All existence centered around the sandy base, the endless desert, and the enemy. Wherever he might be. Bombing missions came up every few days, some that never made the papers back in the states. Insurgents acting up or strategic military sites belonging to start-up terrorist groups. The Air Force handled strikes, but the choppers came in before and after, dropping supplies or men to aid in the attack. Air attacks made up a routine part of their work.

Always there were dangerous missions. And that Sunday, December 11, two weeks before Christmas, the mission that lay ahead was the most dangerous of all.

In the end, the conversation had been short. He had gone in to see his commanding officer, determined that he wouldn't leave the man's presence until he'd been granted permission to man the mission—the one that would have him hovering over an insurgent compound for eleven insane minutes.

"Sir," Mike had stood at attention, his hands at his sides, chin up. "I request permission along with CJ to crew the chopper for the mission."

His superior had mumbled something profane and leaned back in his seat. "I can't afford to lose you, Meade."

"You won't, sir." Mike kept his shoulders straight, his voice even. "Ceej and I can get the job done."

"What about the others? Wouldn't one of them work?"

Mike had held his breath. Some men were dispensable, right? "Sir, the others have much more to lose. CJ and I, we don't have family, sir."

"Fine, Meade." The colonel swore again. He grabbed his pack of cigarettes from the desk and tapped it. "Listen. I didn't ask for this mission, and I can't say I agree with it. The command came from higher up, so someone's got to do it." He snatched a cigarette, slipped it between his lips, and stared at Mike. "But no unnecessary bravery, got it? If you have to pull out and come back, do it. Just get the job done and get out."

Mike could still feel the fire inside his gut at the victory. He stifled a smile. "Yes, sir."

"And follow orders." The man's voice was louder, gruff. He lit the cigarette and inhaled deep. The smoke curled out from the corners of his lips. "The first order most of all."

"The first order, sir?"

"Yes, Meade." He lowered the cigarette. "Come back alive."

Now Mike took another bite of chicken. It was cooler. He studied the picture on the TV screen. The Duke was on horseback, charging ahead, rifle at his side. The movie was just starting to look familiar when one of the chopper pilots walked up and flipped the channel.

"Hey." A soldier jumped up. His coffee spilled, soaking into the dirt. "I was watching that."

"Tough." The man at the set pointed to the man's coffee and laughed out loud. "Looks like you got enough trouble all by your lonesome."

The soldier kicked his coffee cup and stormed off. Mike looked at the airman again. He was still flipping channels. Mike thought about saying something. The Duke was about to do in a few bad guys, after all. But he stared at his chicken instead. TV didn't matter. He needed a clear head if he was going to get the mission underway and come out breathing.

"Country videos?" The soldier was back with a new cup. He sat down and kicked his feet out. "What'd you go wussy on us, man? Come on! You turned off the Duke!"

"Look," the pilot raised his hand in the air. "None of yer bellyaching now, y'hear? I'm country folk myself, and my sweet little wife back in Alabama has a message comin' to me on one of these videos." He grinned, and a few of the guys seated around the television chuckled and muttered under their breath, guessing at the content of the message. The pilot waved off the comments. "We're watchin' country videos until I see the message. Period."

The soldier made a face and sipped his drink. "Wussies, all of you."

Another round of laughter as the pilot found the right channel. He turned the volume up and took the chair closest to the set, arms crossed, expectant.

Mike laughed to himself. Stations running those sorts of messages had hundreds on every day. He took another bite and shoved a chunk of bread into his mouth. Probably the last full meal he'd have for twenty-four hours, by the time they debriefed after the mission.

Across the tent the pilot was talking to the television. "No, not that message, man! Come on! My wife's got the best message of all. Now, please . . . put hers on the stupid screen, y'hear?"

The videos were numbing. Tim McGraw crooning something about a bull ride, and Rascal Flatts singing about today. The songs blended together and Mike helped himself to a second bowl of chicken. He was halfway done when Lonestar kicked in with their classic, *Already There.*

At that exact moment something caught his eye.

The pilot was shouting at the TV again, telling the screen to get it right, get his wife's message up. But this message was from a child. That much was obvious because it started out, "Daddy . . ."

The next part made his heart slip all the way down to his dirty boots.

In plain text along the right side of the video, the message read:

> *Daddy, this is Hannah. Mom showed me the pictures, the one with me and you reading and the other one, with you and your surfboard. I'm trying to find you. So if you*

see this, call the station and they'll tell you how to reach me. I love you, Daddy. I never forgot you. Hannah.

Mike lifted slowly from his chair and stared at the television. *Hannah?* His Hannah? Could it really be? He read the message again, the part about the girl's mother showing her pictures, and how they read books, and the surfboard. The video ended then, and without taking his eyes from the screen, Mike tossed his plate. He reached the pilot near the television in three giant strides. "What station is it?"

"Huh?"

"The station," Mike pointed at the TV. "What station is it?"

The pilot rattled off the name. Mike was gone before the last word was out.

Hannah remembered him.

He had to call. Colonel Whalin was at his desk when Mike walked in, breathless. "Colonel . . ." He straightened, at attention. "I need a favor."

The man was between cigarettes. "Don't tell me." He gave a wry grin. "You want out of the mission?"

Mike hesitated. If it was his Hannah and she was looking for him, then . . . He pressed his shoulders back some more. The mission was his, no matter what. "No, sir. I need to make a couple of calls to the States."

His commander was lenient with stateside calls. The regularly scheduled ones came often—especially for the family guys. He slid the phone across the desk. "You know the codes?"

"Yes, sir." Mike only knew them from checking on his house in Pismo Beach. Personal calls didn't happen.

"Go ahead." The officer stood, stretched, and headed out the tent door. "I need fresh air, anyway."

"Thank you, sir."

Mike worked fast, his first call to a buddy back at the base stateside. He'd need to use that number if Hannah was to call him. She'd call the base, talk to his buddy, and be patched in to the colonel's office in Baghdad.

Next he found the television station's number. It had to be her, didn't it? How many Hannahs had a lost father who surfed? His palms were sweating by the time a person finally answered at the station. "Hi . . ." He was short of breath. "I'm looking for the person who takes the messages, the ones for servicemen."

"Just a minute, please."

Mike gripped the phone, his posture stiff. Was he crazy? Had the desert heat and sand finally gotten to him? Or was it the mission? He'd looked for Hannah all those years. What were the odds he'd get his first clue the night before the most dangerous job he'd ever taken?

He braced himself against the desk. *Come on . . . Someone pick up . . .*

His commander was talking to a few men just outside the tent. He didn't have long by himself. Mike tapped his foot. *Come on and—*

"Hello . . . this is the message department, can I help you?" The woman on the other end sounded busy.

"Yes, ma'am." He raked his fingers across his short cut hair. How did he say this? "Okay . . . I'm an Army chopper pilot in Iraq, and I just saw a message on one of your videos."

"Good." Her voice softened. "You're the reason we have the messages. How are things in Iraq?"

Details of the next day's mission flashed in his mind. "Fine. Just fine." He worked the muscles in his jaw. "Listen, ma'am, a minute ago the message . . . It was from a girl named Hannah. She's looking for her dad." He paused. There was no turning back now. "I think she might be looking for me."

"Really? Let me write this down."

"Yes, if you could." He only had a few minutes of privacy left. "My name's Mike Meade. I'm stationed outside Baghdad in Iraq, and I've been looking for my daughter, Hannah, for eleven years." He waited. There was no sound of typing in the background. He turned around and rested against the desk. Was she scribbling it on a scrap piece of paper? "Got that, ma'am?"

"Yes." She sounded distracted. "How can she reach you?"

Mike gave her the base number, the one that would put her in to his buddy. "Ask her to have them patch her in to Colonel Jared Whalin's office in Baghdad."

"Okay." A few seconds passed. "There. You're Mike

Meade, you've been looking for a daughter named Hannah for eleven years, and you're in Baghdad."

"Right." He searched his mind. "One more thing." He hesitated. "I used to surf."

"Surf?"

"Yes, ma'am. It was part of the message on the video. She has a picture of her father with a surfboard."

"Well," the woman's tone was hopeful. "Maybe you're the one."

"I hope so. You'll make sure she gets the message?"

"I will. I'll look up her information and give her a call within the hour. So if I give her the number you gave me, she'll be patched through to you?"

"Yes, ma'am." Mike had no doubts. Colonel Whalin would walk through fire to give him the message if his daughter called for him.

"Very good, then. I'll do my best."

"Thank you, ma'am."

The conversation ended just as his commanding officer returned to his desk. "Take care of everything?"

"Yes, sir." Mike stood at attention again. "Something personal."

The man motioned to him. "At ease, Meade."

Mike relaxed. "I'm ready, sir. Everything's in order."

"Good." He looked down, took hold of the ashtray on his desk, and gave it a light shake. The soft gray ashes inside fell to an even layer. "Look, Meade, we've done everything we can to minimize the danger." He glanced up. "But it's still a risk. You'll be hanging in the air a long time."

"I know, sir." Mike tried to concentrate, but he kept hearing her voice. *"You and me, Daddy. This'll be our house someday . . ."*

Colonel Whalin anchored his forearms on his desk. "Your guard has to be up every minute, every second."

"Yes, sir." She was drawing him the picture with the big yellow sun, writing her first sentence. *Hannah loves Daddy.* He squinted. "Every second."

"Take no chances, Meade. Everything by the book."

"Of course, sir." And she was in his arms, cuddling with him while he read *The Cat in the Hat Comes Back* and giggling when the cat ate pink cake in the tub and . . .

"No chances at all, Meade, you understand?"

"Yes, sir." And now there was the slightest small chance that she remembered him, that she was looking for him the same way he'd been looking for her. That he might see her again. "No chances at all."

Colonel Whalin rapped the desk and pushed his chair back. "I'll be out there tomorrow to see you off. And one more thing . . ." He searched Mike's eyes. "We'll have Air Force medevac on standby. Just in case."

"Yes, sir." The news was good, but it underlined the obvious. A mission like this came with an expected number of wounded men. Possibly even casualties. "Thank you, sir."

"Go get some sleep."

Mike started to go, but he hesitated. "Sir . . . I might get a phone call tonight. It's, well," he scratched his head. "It's important, sir."

The colonel looked at him for a long moment. "I'll get you, Meade. Whatever the hour, I'll get you."

As soon as he was back at his bunk, Mike pulled out the bag. It was still early, and he was alone in his area of the tent. He eased the contents out onto his bed and let his fingers move slowly over them. The broken clay pieces, the delicate folded paper, the photo of him and Hannah building a sandcastle on the beach.

"Hannah . . ." He let her name settle on his lips, the way it had so often back when she was his. Her eyes seemed to look straight to his soul, and he moved his finger over her hair, her face. "Hannah girl, I love you."

He looked at the items for a long time, and put them away just before the other men filed into the tent a few at a time and prepared for bed.

CJ approached him first. He sat on the edge of his cot and gave his socked foot a squeeze. "We'll be okay. I have a good feeling about it."

Mike nodded, fear far from him. "Definitely. No fear, no failure."

"Right." He grinned. CJ was long and lanky with an easy smile, even in the most tense situations. "I figure eleven minutes in the air isn't too bad. Remember the Gulf War? What'd we hang there for, half an hour that one time?"

A smile tugged at the corners of Mike's mouth. "I think it was eight minutes."

"Ah, you know . . ." CJ leaned back on his elbows. "Eight minutes, thirty minutes. Same thing, right?"

Mike thought about the brown bag beneath his cot. "All in a day's work."

"Right." CJ winked at him and jumped up, headed off to his own cot and whatever he still needed to get in order for the mission.

Jimbo and Fossie took turns talking to him after that, laughing about some joke they'd heard in the food tent.

"Hey, man, be careful out there." Jimbo gave him a light punch in the shoulder. "We need you."

"You know it." Mike still had the bag in front of him, his fingers tight around the neck. "Don't give my bed away. CJ's, either."

"You'll be back tomorrow night."

"But if I'm not." He gave Jimbo an easy smile. A mission like this came with the possibility of capture. "You know. Just don't give my bed away."

"Never."

Fossie was next, handling his good-bye the same, keeping things light. He patted Mike's stomach with the back of his hand. "Nerves of steal, Meade. Same as back in your surfing days, right? Catch a wave and ride it home."

Mike chuckled. "Hadn't thought of that."

"See . . ." He grinned. "That's why they call me Fossie the Optimist."

The other guys made a point of saying something, both to him and to CJ. Wishing him luck or the best or whatever it is guys say when they know there's a chance they won't see each other again. Only Stoker mentioned prayer.

"You a praying kind of guy, Mike?" Stoker pulled up a chair and turned it around, sitting so that his arms rested on the back.

Mike shrugged. "Sometimes more than others."

"Me, too." Stoker shrugged. "I guess it's never a perfect science."

"No." Mike glanced at his watch. It had been an hour and still she hadn't called. *Come on, Hannah . . . pick up the phone and dial the number.*

"Anyway, I want to promise you something."

"What?"

"I'll pray for you, Meade. The whole time you're gone."

"Okay." Was it the danger ahead or the video message from a girl named Hannah? Mike wasn't sure, but the idea of Stoker praying for him made something inside him relax a little. He smiled at his friend. "Don't forget."

Stoker stood and turned the chair back around. "I won't."

It took another hour for the guys in his tent to fall asleep. All but him. She still hadn't called, and that could only mean a few possibilities. Either she wasn't home, or she wasn't the right Hannah.

And as the night wore on, as ten o'clock became midnight and midnight became two, and the mission drew closer, Mike forced himself to fall asleep. Because he couldn't be on his guard unless he got some rest, and if he wasn't on his guard he wouldn't come back alive.

Which was something he had to do. Not just because it was Colonel Whalin's order, but because Hannah might be looking for him, because she might still remember him. That fact and the image of a little girl who still lived in his memory would be enough to keep him alert and ready at all times.

Even on the most dangerous mission of all.

❧

At eleven o'clock that night in Nashville, Tennessee, an evening janitor made his way into the studio of the nation's biggest country western music television station and began cleaning around a bank of computers. The room was empty except for a few producers working on feature pieces.

As was his routine every night, he sprayed a fine mist of industrial cleaner on the desktop around the computers and rubbed away the day's grime and germs. The producers and staff assistants at the station knew to keep loose notes and scrap papers in their desk drawers and normally he could clean around whatever stacks of information or files or documents might be shoved up against the computer screens.

But this night—as was the case on occasion—when the janitor rubbed his rag across the desktop, a single piece of notepaper drifted to the floor. The janitor stopped, straightened, and pressed his fist into the small of his back. He'd been cleaning offices for twenty-two years. His body was feeling the effects.

He set the rag down, bent over, picked up the piece of notepaper, and stared at it. The words were scribbled and hard to read. Something about Mike Meade and surfing and someone named Hannah. A phone number was written across the bottom. The janitor studied it a moment longer and turned back to the row of computer stations.

Where had the paper fallen from? Had it been near the computer on the end, or the one in from that? Or possibly the computer four stations down? The janitor shrugged, opened the desk drawer closest to him, and tossed the paper inside.

Someone would find it eventually.

CHAPTER SEVEN

$\mathcal{C}$arol Roberts boarded a plane bound for Washington, D.C., late Tuesday night, December 13. Her frustration was at an all-time high. She hadn't wanted to come home during the holiday season, but now she had no choice. Four days had passed since bedlam broke loose in the States, since the *Washington Post* ran an article under the headline, "Daughter of Former Senator Searches for Biological Father."

The plane was crowded, but Carol barely noticed. From her seat in first class, she stared out the window, closed her eyes, and pressed her forehead against the cool glass. What was Hannah thinking? The letter hadn't been for anyone's eyes but hers. She was supposed to read it, take in the information, and squirrel it away somewhere. It was supposed to occupy her mind and make the holidays less lonely.

Since then the story had run in every major news-

paper in the United States, including *USA Today*. None of
the reporters were pointing fingers at Carol or Jack. Instead it had become a human interest story: "Will Ambassador's Daughter Find Birth Father in Time for
Christmas?" One paper wrote an emotional plea for the
man to surface under the headline: "Hannah's Hope—
will Christmas Include a Visit from Her Father?"

The media circus had made its way to Sweden, dou-
bling the calls that normally came from the U.S. to the
embassy. Reporters wanted to know what was being done
from the ambassador's office to help find Mike Conner.
And what was the reason Hannah was only finding out
about him now? And how come Carol had left him when
he joined the Army? And had he really joined the Army,
since no record had been found indicating the truth in
that?

Finally Jack had given her an order. "Get home and
take care of this mess. We can't afford the distraction."

Carol clenched her fists. Jack was right, and that's why
she was on a plane headed for Washington, D.C. A dull
ache pounded in her temples. If Hannah wanted help
finding Mike Conner, why hadn't she simply called? Carol
might not have had all the answers, but she could've put
Hannah in touch with someone who did. Instead the girl
had shown the independence that had marked her recent
years.

Calling Congressman McKenna? What fifteen-year-
old did things like that? And granting an interview with

the *Washington Post*? Carol repositioned herself, settling against the headrest. She kept her eyes closed. The next two weeks were supposed to be spent planning parties and receptions and dinners for dignitaries.

Since the news had broke, the conversations with Hannah had been short. The last one, two days earlier, was what finally convinced her to board the plane. She needed to get back to the States and cool things off. For everyone's sake. Carol let the words play in her mind again . . .

"The *Washington Post*? How could you, Hannah?"

"You're repeating yourself, Mother."

"I'll repeat myself as much as I like." Carol had been pacing across the Italian stone floor in her spacious kitchen. "The *Washington Post*? Do you realize what you've done?"

"What, Mother? What have I done?" Hannah's voice rang out, shrill and sincere. "You mean by telling the truth?" She exhaled hard and fast. "Well, maybe I'm not much of a liar. Can you imagine that? Maybe I think it's better to be honest."

"Your father is a very important man." Carol hissed the words. "He doesn't need our name plastered over every newspaper in the country."

"My father is missing. Isn't that the point?"

"Our family life is no one's business but ours." Carol heard the lack of compassion in her voice. "The world doesn't need to know about Mike Conner."

"Yes." The fight left Hannah. "But *he* needs to know." She made a sniffing sound. "Otherwise I'll never find him."

"What's the rush, Hannah?" A calm came over Carol. She was angry at Hannah, but she hadn't meant to make her daughter cry. "He's been out of your life for more than a decade. Why do you have to find him now?"

"Because." She coughed twice, her words thick. "Because I want to spend Christmas with him."

That was when Carol knew she'd have to go home. Her plan had backfired. She had hoped the information about Mike would distract Hannah, keep her mind occupied so she wouldn't be bored during the holidays. But she never should've said anything, never should've told her. Not until she was older. Because now the whole world knew about Mike Conner.

As the flight got underway, Carol tried to sleep, but all she could think about was a blond, blue-eyed surfer and whether right now, somewhere in the world, he knew that Hannah's single hope was to find him before December 25. Like gathering storm clouds, other details about her time with Mike built along her heart's horizon. She held them off while they crossed the Atlantic and as they landed at Dulles International Airport just before noon Wednesday. She kept them at bay on the limo ride to her house and even as she came through the front door and greeted her mother.

There was no need to talk about the subject. Obviously she'd come home to clear up the media disaster. Her mother only raised her brow and gave the slightest shake of her head. "Why did you tell her?"

Carol looked away. "She had to know sometime."

"Yes, in person, maybe. When she would have been old enough to sort through the news."

Carol's anger bubbled closer to the surface. "Thank you, Mother. I'll handle it from here."

And that was all there was. After a few minutes, her mother returned to her room. Two hours later when she appeared downstairs again, she was stiff and distant, her chin tilted upward, eyes narrow. "Have you called Hannah?"

"Not yet."

"Call her. I'll have lunch for us in the dining room."

Carol studied her mother, watched as she turned, back straight, and headed for the kitchen. When had things between them grown so shallow and cold? A functional ability to exist in the same room was all they had together, all they shared. But even as she pondered the lack of depth between her and her mother, a question slammed into her soul.

Was this how Hannah saw her? An imposing figure who visited a few times a year? Suddenly the cost of living overseas felt overwhelming. What had she missed with Hannah? Walks in the park and bedtime stories? Endless conversations about school and boys and maybe even Mike Conner? Certainly his place in her life would've come up sooner if she and Hannah lived together.

Carol dismissed the thoughts. She spun, walked down the hall and into their home office, and shut the double doors. Hannah's cell phone would be off during school hours. She went to the phone and dialed the school's number.

"Thomas Jefferson Prep, how can I help you?"

"This is Carol Roberts." Carol leaned against the desk and felt the tension at the base of her neck. Maybe Hannah wouldn't care if she was home; maybe she'd disregard her request and stay at school all afternoon. Carol summoned her strength. The clouds in her memory were about to break wide open. "I need to get a message to my daughter, Hannah. She's a freshman."

※※※

*H*annah was in advanced placement history that afternoon sitting next to the jerky junior, the one with blond hair, when an office attendant came through the door and whispered something to the teacher. After a few seconds the teacher nodded his head and took a note from the attendant.

As the woman left, the teacher looked at Hannah. "Ms. Roberts, I have a note for you."

A note? Hannah felt her back tense. Could it be from Mike Conner? Had he seen the story and found her at TJ Prep? Who else would be sending her a note in the middle of the school day? She gulped and straightened herself in her chair, her eyes on the paper in the teacher's hand.

"Hey, Hannah." The blond next to her leaned in. "Secret admirers in the office, too?" His tone was ripe with teasing. "So what's wrong with me, Hannah? I could help you find your dad."

"You—" She made a face at him, her voice louder than she intended. "—are pathetic. You couldn't help me find my way out of the room."

The teacher rapped his hand on the closest wall. "Classroom visitors," his voice boomed across the room, "are no excuse for childish behavior." He gave a sharp look at the junior and then at Hannah. "Miss Roberts, you will refrain from any further outbursts."

Hannah's hands trembled as she took the note from the teacher. She gave the blond one last glare. Everyone knew about her father now, but she didn't care. He had to be out there somewhere, seeing the stories, watching the music video with her message. Any day now he was bound to get in touch with her.

She opened the paper slowly, like it was a bad report card. Her eyes skipped to the bottom of the wording, and what she read there made the blood drain from her face. What was this? The note wasn't from her father at all. It was from her mother: *Darling . . . I'm at home waiting for you. Cancel your afternoon appointments. We need to talk. Mother.*

Hannah stared at the words. She read them two more

times, folded the note, and slipped it into her backpack. The jerky junior was staring at her, and she didn't want to tip him off, didn't want him to know that the note had upset her.

Her mother was home? All the way from Sweden? For a fraction of an instant, Hannah wanted to believe she'd come because of her request—that she be home for Christmas. After all, Buddy Bingo was praying every day for a Christmas miracle, so that Hannah could spend the holidays with her mom and dad.

But that wasn't why her mother had come. Of course not. She'd come because of the newspaper stories, because her own reputation was on the line. Hannah quietly seethed. Her mother cared nothing about being together for the holidays, but when her own public image was threatened, she'd get on a plane practically without notice and fly all day if she had to.

Three hours later—after talking with her cheer coach and her dance instructor—Hannah walked out the doors of TJ Prep. She'd told Buddy Bingo about the change in plans. He'd be there by now.

But instead, as she headed down the brick-lined walkway toward the circular drive and parent pick-up area, she saw her mother's sporty silver Jag. Hannah's steps slowed. Her mother had come? Were they headed straight for the office of the *Washington Post*?

She bit her lip and kept walking. Whatever her mother wanted from her, she wasn't about to cooperate. Not until her mother helped her find her dad. Hannah reached the car, opened the door, and slid inside. Without looking at her mom she said, "Hello, Mother. Thank you for picking me up." Formalities came first in the Roberts family. She set her backpack on the floor of the car and turned to meet her mother's eyes. "Can I ask why you're here?"

Her mother leaned back against the headrest, her gaze locked on Hannah's. Something in her eyes was different, softer. Instead of rattling off a list of things they were going to accomplish, instead of slipping the car into gear and driving away without so much as a glance in Hannah's direction, her mother gave her a sad sort of look.

"I'm here—" She reached out and touched Hannah's shoulder. "—because I want to tell you about Mike Conner."

CHAPTER EIGHT

*W*ith every moment, every step, Carol could feel the years slipping away.

They went to a coffee shop, a dimly lit place tucked between the Yarn Barn and a Geoffrey Allen hair salon in an older section of Bethesda. At three-thirty in the afternoon they were the only customers. They ordered—a nonfat, sugar-free vanilla latte for Carol, a caramel macchiato for Hannah—and took their drinks to a booth at the back of the room.

The entire time, Carol watched Hannah with new eyes. A long time ago, she'd been just like her, hadn't she? Independent, indifferent to the political importance of her parents, articulate beyond her years. Her father had been a congressman, and her mother had planned out Carol's life long before she entered high school.

They sat across from each other and Carol stirred her

drink. "Mike was everything I couldn't have," she said without explanation.

"Really?" Hannah's eyes were wide. She looked nervous, expectant, like she was afraid to breathe for fear Carol would change her mind.

Carol sipped her coffee. Her eyes found a place at the center of her drink. "After high school I went to Pismo Beach with my best friend, Clara. Her aunt and uncle lived there." Carol's vision blurred and she could see Clara again, feel the excitement of getting away from Washington, D.C., going somewhere as foreign and exotic as California. She looked up at Hannah. "I met Mike on the beach the second day of summer."

"What was he like?"

Carol smiled. "He was the most handsome boy on the beach. Tan and blond, muscled from years of surfing." Carol looked at the table, the past clearer still. "He saw Clara and me on our towels and came over. His hair was wet." She touched her eyebrows. "Drops of salt water hung on his eyelashes and from the tip of his nose. He had a beat-up surfboard under one arm." She uttered a single chuckle at the image in her memory. "He said he was giving surfing lessons if we wanted to learn."

"That's so cool."

Carol smiled and found Hannah's eyes again. "It was."

A spark lit in Hannah's eyes. She was engaged now, fully caught up in the story. Carol settled against the back of the booth and allowed the story to come in rich detail, the way it had felt all those years ago . . .

❧

 $\mathcal{W}$ ith Mike standing on the hot sand a few feet from them, hand outstretched, Carol looked at Clara and shrugged. Then she took Mike's hand, let him pull her to her feet, and ran after him toward the surf.

She'd never stepped foot in the Pacific Ocean, let alone been on a surfboard. But Mike was tall and confident, strong in a way that felt safe and dangerous all at the same time.

"So," he looked over his shoulder at her as they hopped the surf and headed out to waist-deep water, "where you from?"

"D.C."

He stopped, the surfboard still under his arm, and gave her a slight grin. "Washington, D.C.?"

"Right." She felt uneasy, as if being from the East Coast meant she somehow didn't measure up.

But he only studied her and said, "I'm Mike Conner."

"I'm Carol. Carol Paul."

"Hi, Carol." He grinned again and gave her hand a quick squeeze. Then he said something that stuck with her for the next few years. "People from Washington, D.C., are too serious."

"Oh, yeah?" She felt her eyes dance, felt them catch a splash of sunshine in the reflection off the water.

"Yeah." He took a few more steps forward, his eyes still on hers. "Way too serious."

"Okay." With her free hand she made a quick skimming motion over the surf, spraying water at his face. "How's that for serious?"

He laughed again, shaking the wetness off his face. "Not bad." He dropped his surfboard in the water and high stepped it through the shallow water until he caught her. Then he gripped her waist, picked her up, and tossed her toward the deeper water.

"Mike!" She was breathless when she came up for air, not so much because of the cold water, but because Mike was standing a few feet away grinning, his chest heaving. "More?"

"No!" She held her hands out, trying to keep him away. "I thought you were teaching me how to surf!"

He held his arms out and laughed again. "But then Miss Serious went and splashed me!" Mike turned and snagged his surfboard, which was drifting away. They were the only ones in that area of the water. "You want a lesson or not?"

Carol blinked and took another sip of her coffee. "I felt free and happy and alive, Hannah." She looked at her daughter. "It was the first time I could remember feeling that way."

Hannah was quiet, waiting for the rest.

"We surfed together the rest of the day." Carol stared at the empty seat beside Hannah. She could see Mike pressing the surfboard down below the water and climbing on top of it, hear him explaining it to her that first time . . .

✦

*Y*ou get on like this, then you paddle to where the waves are breaking." He pointed to an area of the ocean a few dozen yards out. "The wave builds up and you paddle like crazy. When you feel the wave catch the board, you pull yourself up onto your feet."

Carol must've looked lost, because Mike chuckled and shook his head. "Scratch that. First time just stay on your stomach and ride it in."

He showed her a few times, and on the third time he slipped his feet beneath him and stood up, easily maneuvering the board through the wave. Before the surf evened out, he saluted her and fell off.

"Your turn." He was dripping wet as he moved gracefully through the water, carrying the surfboard to her. She took the board and he looped his arm around her waist, holding the board steady while she climbed on. Her heart pounded within her; she was terrified that a shark would snatch her feet or that a big wave would pull her out to deep water, never to be seen or heard from again.

But Mike shouted at her from his place in the shallow surf, telling her when to turn around, when to paddle hard, and she caught the first wave that came her way. The speed gave her a rush she hadn't expected. She flew on the board across the water, not stopping until the wave died and the board spilled her into the knee-deep tide.

She hooted and raised her fist, pumping it in the air. Out where he stood in the water, Mike did the same. And in that moment, she forgot completely about her parents' politics or the expectations her mother had for her.

All that mattered was Mike Conner and the way he made her feel.

They spent the day in the water. Every now and then Clara would come close to the water, sometimes close enough to get her toes wet. "Carol," she'd holler across the sound of the surf. "You're gonna get sunburned."

"I'm fine," Carol would shout back.

And in that way she stayed out in the water with Mike until the afternoon sun was heading fast for the horizon. Mike walked with her back to the towel, looking at her the whole time. "How old are you?"

She was glad for the sunshine, glad he couldn't see the heat in her cheeks from his nearness and the bold way he had with her. "Nineteen this fall," she told him. "You?"

"Twenty-one." He seemed to anticipate her next question. He spread his hand out and gestured to the sandy beach. "This is my office."

"Your office?" She giggled.

"I'm a lifeguard." The two of them still made their

way up the sand toward where Clara was reading. He winked at her. "Today's my day off."

Carol didn't let her surprise show. Every boy that age back home—the ones in her circle, anyway—were working on their bachelor's degree, making plans to intern in someone's office or for someone's campaign. She couldn't imagine spending every day on a beach.

Just before they reached Clara and the towels, Mike turned to her and took her hand. "Go out with me tonight. We'll get some ice cream, maybe, and come back here, okay?" He gazed out to sea. "It's beautiful at night."

She'd been wondering if she would see him again. And in that moment, his words came back to her. *"People from Washington, D.C., are too serious."* She swallowed her fears and nodded big. "Clara won't mind."

Clara didn't, but her parents did. They asked Mike to come in when he stopped by to pick her up that night. After chatting with him for ten minutes they gave a nod in Carol's direction. It was okay; she could go out with him.

That night, when their ice cream was gone, Mike took her to a pier not far from the beach where they'd played earlier that day. They walked to the end and leaned against the old wooden railing.

"See?" He faced her, his elbow looped casually over the rail. "Isn't it beautiful?"

It was. Carol had never felt so free and alive and . . . and something else. She was trying to figure it out when he leaned in and kissed her.

School and political functions and vacations to the eastern seaboard had made up Carol's entire life until that point. She had never been kissed, and the feel of it—sweet and full and brief—made her wonder if she could ever go back.

She paced herself after that, spending half her time with Clara, and half with Mike. He had a friend, and several times a week the four of them would double date.

Partway through summer, her mother confronted her about the situation.

"Clara's mother tells me you've found a boy."

"Yes." Carol cringed. The way her mother said it, *boy* sounded like a contagious disease. "Yes." She tried to salvage the situation. "His name is Mike. He's very nice."

"He's a . . . surfer, is that it?"

"He protects people at the beach. It's a very honorable job, Mother."

"Carol, what would you know about honorable." Her mother was disgusted, the pretense gone. "Lifeguards are drifters."

"He's not a drifter. He's kind and funny and he makes me smile."

"This conversation is over." Her mother was hissing now, furious. "You won't see the boy again, is that understood? You have college and half a dozen wonderful young men waiting for you here at home. People like us don't date surfers, Carol." She huffed for emphasis. "Am I understood?"

Carol had nothing to say to her. She hung up before her mother could finish. She had no intention of following orders this time. She couldn't follow them if she wanted to. Because by then she'd fallen for Mike—fallen hard, the same way he had.

"Summer's almost over," he told her one night as they walked along the beach. He turned and searched her eyes. "Stay with me, Carol. Marry me. No one's ever made me feel this way."

Two thoughts hit Carol at the same instant: first, she would stay. How could she do anything else? But the other thought caught her off guard. She didn't want to marry him. Marriage meant a wedding, the sort that involved a year of planning and a beautiful gown and a dinner party with hundreds of important people. Those were the only weddings she knew, and if she ever got married, that would be the type she would have.

But if she married Mike Conner, she might as well elope. Her parents wouldn't come to the wedding. They'd hardly throw her a party.

"Well . . ." He slipped his hands in his pocket and gave a shrug of his shoulders. He had never looked more irresistible. Then he pulled a ring from his pocket, a slender solitaire with a small diamond at the center. He held it out to her, his eyes damp. "Will you marry me, Carol?"

"Mike . . . yes!" A soft gasp came from her and she let him slip the ring on her finger. Her brain was shouting at her, telling her it could never work with her parents so set against it. But in that moment she wanted only to be in Mike's arms, lost in his embrace, his kiss.

✻❦✻

*C*arol stopped talking and looked at her coffee. It was half full, too cold to drink. She looked at Hannah. "I never had time to think it through." She gave a light shrug. "When Mike gave me the ring, I figured it didn't matter. The world could fall apart and I'd be okay as long as I had him in my life."

"So . . . you did marry him?"

"No." Carol looked down at her fingers, at the ring on her left hand, the ring from Jack Roberts. She drew in a slow breath and met Hannah's curious eyes once more. "I called my parents the next day to tell them the news. They said if that was my decision, they would wash their hands of me."

Hannah took another swig from her drink. "I can picture Grandmother doing that."

The remark cut at Carol. Wasn't it the same thing she would've done if Hannah had called with a similar pronouncement? She leaned back, missing Mike for the first time in years. "I moved in with him." She pursed her lips and shrugged. "Not very smart, but that's what I did. I enrolled in a local college and every month or so I promised him we'd get married soon." She anchored her elbows on the table and gave Hannah a sad smile. "Instead, I wound up pregnant with you."

"What did . . . what did Mike think?"

"He was thrilled. He said it was the perfect reason to get married, now that we were going to be a family."

"Did Grandmother and Grandfather know?"

"I called and told them." Carol remembered their voices, the disappointment. "They told me they'd be waiting for me in Washington, D.C., if I ever got smart and decided to come home." She paused, the memories alive again. "Mike was a wonderful father." She looked at Hannah. "Better at parenting than I was, I'm afraid."

Hannah stirred the straw in her drink. "I remember him." She squinted, and it looked like she was fighting tears. "Did I ever tell you that?"

"No." Carol felt her heart skip a beat. Hannah remembered? No wonder the package had set her off, caused her to go on a frantic search for him. "What do you remember?"

Hannah looked up at nothing in particular. "I remember sitting and playing on the floor with him." Her eyes met Carol's. "I remember him playing the guitar."

"Yes." Carol's throat was thick. "He was quite good."

"So what happened?" Hannah's voice was thick. Tears filled her eyes. "Why did you leave?"

Carol squirmed, but there was no comfortable way to say it. "I grew ambitious, dreaming about the sort of life I'd lived as a kid. The successful politicians, the savvy businessmen, the wealth and privilege, I began to crave it all. Mike wasn't . . . He wasn't enough after awhile." Her heart wanted her to regret the decision, but she couldn't. The truth was she'd leave him again if she had it to do over.

She clenched her teeth, not sure how to go on. But after a few seconds she summed up the ending. Mike had wanted to give Carol the life she hungered after, but he wasn't able. He was a lifeguard—a happy, kind man who would never be invited to high-powered political parties, never provide a six-figure income for his family.

By the time Hannah was three, Mike became insistent that they get married. "This is no life for a little girl, Carol," he would tell her. "We need to give her security, a real life. I don't want her to think of me as her mother's boyfriend."

Carol refused, insisting that she couldn't commit a lifetime to him unless he had some other direction for his future, something other than guarding Pismo Beach.

"That's lousy, Mother." Hannah's voice was just short of condemning.

"I know it." Carol deserved this, deserved the pain in her heart that came from talking about the past, from admitting her part in it all. "It was very lousy."

Hannah played with her straw some more, her eyes never leaving Carol's. "So what happened?"

"He enlisted with the Army. He wanted to fly planes, but he didn't have a college degree. So he joined the Army. That way he could be a helicopter pilot. A warrant officer. Something he thought would carry the prestige and future I wanted." Carol pressed her fingertips to her eyes, warding off the headache that was starting near her temples. "He absolutely enlisted. I'm sure of it."

"They can't find his records. I had them check every branch for Mike Conner."

"Wait." Carol's eyes narrowed. "*Conner* wasn't his given name. It might've been his middle name, actually." She closed her eyes, willing herself to remember. Suddenly it came to her. "His legal name was Mike Meade. Mike Conner Meade. I'll bet he's enlisted under that name."

Life sprang to Hannah's eyes. "Really?"

"Yes." Carol was catching Hannah's enthusiasm. "On the beach he went by Conner. It was his middle name. The guys called him Mike Conner. Almost no one knew him by his last name."

"It's worth checking." Hannah's expression came to life again. "Maybe when we get home, okay?"

"Okay." Carol's stomach tightened. Was it possible? Would they really find Mike, and if a visit was arranged, would she be able to look him in the eyes after so many years?

Hannah leaned in, her eyes sad. "Was it hard? Saying good-bye to my dad?"

Carol felt her chin quiver. "I loved him, Hannah. I didn't know how much until I left him." She hesitated. The headache was getting worse. "But it was harder on you."

A memory drifted back. Mike had his things in order for basic training, the period that would take him away for as much as four months . . .

❦

"Wait for me, Carol." He'd found her outside staring at the sky that night. He positioned himself in front of her and put his hands on her shoulders. "Please. You and Hannah. Let me get through training, then we'll live on base and after a few years we'll make our way back here, to the beach."

But she shook her head. By then her mind was made up. Her mother was right; her kind was in Washington, D.C. She'd been tricking herself all those years, but no more. "I can't stay here, Mike. Hannah and I are going home. At least for now."

In the end there was nothing Mike could do. He begged her to stay in the beach house, begged her every day. But she left one morning after he left for Oklahoma. There were a few more conversations, and lots of questions from Hannah. But neither of them ever saw Mike Conner Meade again.

❦

Carol took a breath. The story was over, there were no more details to share, no more anecdotes to remember.

"What about me?" Hannah's voice cracked, fresh tears on her cheeks.

Carol reached across the table and took hold of her daughter's hands, which after so much time apart didn't feel even a little bit familiar. "You . . . you cried for days, weeks." It hurt worse now, remembering how it felt to leave Mike, how it had been to watch Hannah fall apart.

Now that the truth was out, tension made the air between them thick. Why had she done it? So she could find a man with money? With political power and connections in the nation's capital? Mike had been so different. He'd taught her how to laugh and spend quiet nights around the fireplace while he played the guitar. He taught her to run carefree down a sandy beach and, for a little while at least, to live free of the expectations of others.

But even so, she was sure of the thought that had struck her earlier in the conversation: if she had it to do over again, she would still leave him. Her life with Mike would never have been enough. She belonged in politics, in powerful circles. She'd been wrong to leave her parents' house, wrong to take up with Mike in the first place. And in that sense, no one could ever be more right for her than Jack Roberts.

"Mother," Hannah didn't blink. "How long before I stopped talking about him. Before I forgot him?"

The answers were harder with every question. "Two years." Guilt hung around Carol's neck like a necklace of bricks. It was all she could do to look at her daughter. "When you turned six, you seemed to forget."

Hannah hung her head. Then slowly she folded her

arms up on the table and buried her face in the crook of her elbow. She made no crying sounds, no noise at all. But her shoulders began to tremble and after a minute, her back shook from the force of her silent sobs.

And that was when Carol knew with absolute certainty that she'd been wrong. Hannah had never forgotten, never stopped caring. She'd never for a moment gotten over the loss of her father. For the first time in eleven years, Carol could see that. Her selfish decision had given her the life she truly wanted, the one she loved. But it had hurt other people—her parents, for sure, and of course Mike. But now she knew the worst part.

She'd hurt Hannah most of all.

CHAPTER NINE

The mission had been postponed.

An intelligence report confirmed that the insurgents had left the compound for what appeared to be a short trip into the city. When they returned, there would be little warning. Mike and CJ, the gunner, and the Rangers had to be ready to go at a moment's notice.

In the days that had passed, there'd been no call from Hannah, and Mike had convinced himself. It was a lark, a fluke, a mistake. Somewhere in the world there was another Hannah with a father serving overseas, a father who used to surf and read to his little girl. Mike had made peace with the reality and he was ready to get the mission underway, ready to eliminate the insurgents.

They knew more about the bad guys now. These weren't only insurgents, but terrorists in training. The most elite and organized of the opposition to freedom in

Iraq. Men who were dangerous and cunning, responsible for the deaths of numerous American and Allied forces. A group who needed to be removed from the theater of war as soon as possible.

And so it came as no shock early on the morning of Thursday, December 15, when Mike woke from a light sleep to see Colonel Whalin standing over him. Mike sat up immediately, working to clear his head. "Sir?"

"Meade, it's time. The others are getting ready."

"Yes, sir."

Mike was up and dressed for flight in a few minutes. When they were ready, Colonel Whalin lined them up for a briefing.

"The insurgents have returned to the compound as of yesterday afternoon. They're tired and asleep—sleeping hard, we believe." He was smoking again, pulling hard on the end of a Camel. He paced a few steps and looked at Mike first. "There won't be a better time than now."

Mike was standing at attention alongside Ceej. The gunner was on CJ's other side, and the Rangers were lined up beside him. It was two o'clock in the morning. Their window was a small one.

Colonel Whalin stopped and put his hands on his hips. "The chopper's ready, men. Any questions?"

Mike gave a slight nod. "Yes, sir. Total time for the mission?"

"It's a thirty-minute flight, ten of it over the enemy lines into the area of insurgents. Add ten or eleven minutes for the mission, and I'd expect you back here in seventy-five minutes. Ninety tops. Nothing more."

"Yes, sir." Mike knew the answer, but he wanted to hear it again. That way he could will himself to believe his commander was right. That in an hour and a half they'd be back in their tents, facing Colonel Whalin, debriefing the events of the mission. Thanking Stoker for praying.

The colonel went over a few other details, items they'd discussed before. Then he flicked his cigarette out through the tent flap and stared at the men. "Are we ready?"

Mike was the captain, the one with the most seniority. He saluted his commander. "Ready, sir."

They were ushered out onto a makeshift tarmac where the helicopter was going through last-minute checks. By the time Mike and CJ took the cockpit, it was fueled and ready to go. The Rangers were armed to the teeth, packing M-16 machine guns and M-9 pistols, along with enough ammo to fight their way out of any firestorm. They had protective chest gear and bulletproof helmets.

The gunner was a guy named Fish, with big eyes and few words. He took the jump seat closest to the open door. Mike went through a series of checks with CJ, and then—with the target insurgent compound keyed in on the radar, they lifted.

Choppers were the best way to pull off a mission like this one. They could hover a few feet above a target, waiting while the ground crew handled the job. But noise was always a factor. There was no way to move a military helicopter into an area without noise.

Mike stayed focused as he moved across the enemy lines. The camps below looked quiet, almost completely dark. They were bound to hear the chopper, but by the time they crawled out of bed Mike and his men would be too far gone to bother with.

"Closing in." CJ stared out the window and checked the points on the radar. A few minutes and we'll be overhead."

"Roger that." Mike narrowed his eyes. The men in the cargo area behind him were quiet, no doubt going through the motions of their assignments. Intelligence reports had helped a great deal. Mike knew exactly which part of the roof to hover above, and the Rangers knew which window to break through. The course on the inside had been marked out also.

If everything went well, they might finish in as few as nine minutes. That's what Mike was pulling for.

"Okay, we're coming up on it." CJ still had the trace of a smile, but his voice was tense, the way it always was in situations like this. He was a great copilot because he left no detail to chance. "See it there . . . just ahead."

Mike could see it, but there was something wrong. They'd been told that the compound would be dark. Tired insurgents, sleeping hard after a several day outing into the city for supplies and weapons. Instead, a fire burned in the center courtyard, and a group of people stood around it. Far more people than the fifteen insurgents they'd been sent in to capture.

"It's an ambush." Mike said the words even as the realization was hitting him. The information must've leaked somehow. Or maybe it wasn't an ambush. Maybe the insurgents weren't sleeping because they were debriefing, planning an attack of their own. Either way, it didn't matter. They weren't only in trouble, they were in danger. "Let's get out of here."

Mike was circling, turning the chopper around, when the first grenade ripped through the side of the aircraft, narrowly missing CJ. The control panel was partially destroyed, but before Ceej could survey the damage, a second grenade tore into the rear blades.

"We're hit! We're hit!" CJ shouted the obvious, doing his job, keeping Mike informed.

"Roger, heading back to camp." Mike shouted the affirmation, but it was wishful thinking. The chopper was mortally wounded, losing air speed and altitude. Mike could hear the Rangers' voices, sharp and intense, making plans for the crash landing that was coming.

"We're in trouble!" CJ stared at the crowd of men running toward the wounded chopper.

"Come on, baby, get us over the line." Mike could feel sweat break out across his forehead and his heart raced. He'd been in more firestorms than he could count, but he'd never been hit like this.

"We're losing speed." CJ's face was pale even in the dark. His eyes darted from what was left of the control panel to Mike, and back to the controls. "We need a landing spot."

The chopper was stuck in a circling motion, unable to move ahead because of the damaged rear blades. Mike fought with the machine but it was no use. Ceej was right. They'd have to land the chopper in enemy territory, in plain sight of the insurgents who had fired the rocket-propelled grenades, full sight of every one of the enemy men gathered around the fire at the compound.

The crash came quickly.

Mike and CJ spotted the field at the same time, a small patch of tumbleweeds and sand with buildings on either side. It was their only choice. He let up on the engine and the chopper sputtered toward the ground. "Prepare for landing," he shouted at the men in the back.

Ceej checked the radar once more. "When we touch down, run north," he craned his neck, yelling at the others. "Run away from the compound."

They were details all of them knew, but in the final minute before the chopper hit the ground, the instructions were all Mike or CJ could do. Mike forced his arms to go limp, something he'd learned in flight school. Relaxed pilots survived more often. *Stay relaxed.*

"Don't tense up!" He screamed at Ceej, and in the last seconds before they hit the ground he wondered if this was it, the end of the road for all of them. His eyes met

CJ's just as the chopper leaned hard to the right and made contact with the field.

The fuselage fell apart, ripping right across the place where CJ sat. His head took most of the force of the crash, and by the time the chopper's engines fell silent, Mike didn't have to ask.

Ceej was dead. Just like that, life one second, death the next.

"No!" Mike unbuckled himself, grabbed the name-and-rank patch off CJ's flight suit, and placed his hand on his friend's damaged head. "No, Ceej . . . I'm sorry. I'm so sorry." He hung his head, hesitating only for a heartbeat. Then he pushed his way into the broken cargo area. The gunner and every Ranger had survived. "Let's go!"

Mike was first out of the open door, but already it was too late. The chopper was surrounded by armed insurgents—angry, shouting profanities, mocking the soldiers. Mike stood in front of the others, guarding them. He raised his hands and made eye contact with the insurgents. "Don't shoot!"

One of the insurgents laughed, and then the mob came at them. They were grabbed and pulled from the scene of the crash, six of their guys to every one of the men in the chopper. The fight was over before it began. In the chaos, Mike heard a few English sentences. The one that came across the clearest told him that the end was near:

"Wait," one of the insurgents shouted. "Don't kill them until they're inside."

But the beatings began long before that. With sticks and clubs and rifle butts, the insurgents attacked Mike and the others, hitting them again and again, forgetting the instructions about waiting until they were inside. Mike closed his eyes and one single thought ran through his head.

Hannah . . . Wherever you are, Hannah, I love you. He could feel her in his arms, feel her head cradled against his chest as he read *Cat in the Hat* to her and—

"You!" someone screamed at him. "Open your eyes!"

He did as he was told, blinking back the blood that was streaming down his forehead into his eyes. The door to the compound was still fifty yards away, and at that instant, Mike saw one of the insurgents run through the crowd and swing a boot toward his face.

Then there was nothing but gritty sand and hot-blinding pain and darkness.

$\mathcal{T}$he clue that Mike Conner's real last name was Meade turned out to be all they needed, and now Hannah had a feeling they were hours away from finding her dad.

Her mother had called Congressman McKenna when they returned home from coffee, but he was out for the day. Now it was Thursday afternoon and she had him on the line.

"You've probably read about Hannah's search." Carol managed a polite laugh. "We didn't mean for it to be a media event, but, well . . . the fact is we need to find him." She explained that they had more information now. Mike Meade, she told him. Could he please check the Army for a Mike Meade?

Hannah barely remembered to breathe as her mother put the call on speaker phone. The congressman was checking. After a minute he returned to the phone.

"That's it," he sounded excited. "Mike Meade, born May 7, 1970."

Hannah's mother hung her head, relief filling in the lines on her forehead. "That's him."

"He's a chopper pilot, a captain." The man hesitated. "Looks like he's been in since 1994. He's stationed over in Baghdad, piloting one of the crews designated to fight insurgents."

Hannah wasn't sure what that meant, but it sounded dangerous. She clutched at her stomach and crossed the room to the bank of windows that looked out over their stately neighborhood. *Daddy, we found you.* Tears stung her eyes. *We found you.*

But what if he was in trouble? Insurgents? Those were the bad guys, right? She pressed her head against the window frame and willed herself to think clearly. It was dangerous, but it would be okay. He'd been doing this for years.

She turned and listened to the conversation. Congressman McKenna was talking.

"I'll contact his commander, get a message to him right away so he can call Hannah. If anything comes up, I'll give you a call."

Her mother rattled off a list of cell phones and contact numbers, in case the congressman couldn't get through on the house line. Then she thanked him and hung up.

Hannah had never felt close to her mother, not as far

back as she could remember. But now—with her father found—she walked back to the place where her mother stood, and without saying a word she fell into her arms. The moment was awkward, but Hannah needed it, anyway.

They were still hugging a minute later when the phone rang. Hannah pulled back, confused. Had the congressman located her father's commander that quickly? She wrapped her arms around her middle again and watched as her mother took the call.

After a few seconds her mother handed the phone over. "It's for you," she mouthed silently. "It's the country music station."

Hannah's breath caught in her throat. So much information at once, she could hardly take it in. She held the phone to her ear. "Hello, this is Hannah."

"Hi, this is Megan, I'm one of the producers working with the video messages for soldiers overseas."

"Hello." Hannah braced herself against the back of the sofa. "Have you heard from my dad?"

"I think so." The woman sighed. "It looks like one of the editorial assistants took a message from a Mike Meade a few days ago. The message was misplaced until today. I'm sorry."

"That's okay." Hannah wanted to rush the woman, get to the good part. "Really, you heard from him?"

"Yes. The man who called said to tell you he has similar pictures." She paused. "Oh, and that he was a surfer at Pismo Beach eleven years ago."

Hannah's head was spinning. Her father had called. It had to be him. He'd seen the video and tried to reach her! She wanted to jump through the roof and fly around the neighborhood. How could it be happening? It was all she could do to stay standing, but the woman was rattling off numbers and she took down the information, thanked her, and hung up the phone.

Then, with only a glance at her mother, she dialed the number she'd been given. A woman answered, and Hannah did as the instructions told. "Could you patch me in to Colonel Jared Whalin, please."

"Yes, just a minute." She was silent for a moment. "It's after midnight there. Maybe you could try tomorrow."

"Please!" Hannah heard the panic in her voice. "It's urgent, ma'am. Could you please try? Someone might be awake, right?"

"Well," the woman hesitated. "All right. If it's urgent, I'll give it a try."

She put Hannah on hold and after a few seconds the phone rang and a man picked up. "Colonel Whalin." His voice was terse.

"Yes . . ." Hannah was shaking. She could be minutes from talking to her father. The entire scene felt unreal, like something from a dream. She steadied herself. "My name's Hannah Roberts, and my father—" She let her eyes meet her mother's. "My father is Mike Meade. He's one of your chopper pilots, I believe."

For a few beats the man said nothing. Then he exhaled slowly. "Hannah . . ." His tone was kinder, but it was heavy. "Your father told me you might call."

"Yes, well . . ." Hannah could barely speak. Was this really happening? After so many years of dreaming about her daddy, had she finally found him? Her words were breathless, stuck in her throat. She forced herself to exhale. "Could I talk to him, sir?"

"Hannah, is your mother there? I have some things I need to tell her."

The colonel's words came at her like some sort of disconnect. What did her mother have to do with the conversation? She wanted to speak to her father. Why didn't the colonel go find him and put him on the phone? "Sir? My mother, sir?"

"Yes." The commander sighed again, but it sounded more like a groan. "Please, Hannah."

"Fine, sir." Hannah held the phone to her mother. She felt faint, her mind swirling with the information. What was wrong? Was there a problem, something the colonel couldn't share with her? She gripped the edge of the sofa back and studied her mother.

"Hello?" Her mother knit her brow together, clearly confused. "This is Carol Roberts, Hannah's mother."

Whatever the colonel told her next, Hannah knew it wasn't good. Her mother's face grew pinched, her eyes watery. She gave the commander their phone number and address, but otherwise she said very little, and then the conversation ended. When she hung up the phone, it took a while before she lifted her eyes to Hannah's.

"What's wrong? Why couldn't he come to the phone? How come the colonel didn't tell me?" Hannah's questions ran together. "What's wrong ? Tell me, please."

Her mother reached for her hands and eased her around the edge of the sofa and onto the cushion. Then she crouched down and searched Hannah's eyes. "He's a prisoner, Hannah. His helicopter was shot down earlier today. They're trying to find a way to rescue him."

The words ripped into her, tearing at her dreams and breaking her heart. She slid off the sofa onto her knees and let her head fall against her mother's knees. "No, Mother . . . No, it can't be true. He was fine when he left me the message."

"The colonel talked about that." Her mother's voice was thick. "Your dad called you on Sunday, a few days before the mission."

Hannah grabbed her mother's arms. She was desperate, frantic. She had to find a way to get to him, to tell him she'd gotten his message. "They have to rescue him now, right now! Before something happens."

"Honey, they're trying." Her mother's eyes filled with tears. "The colonel said they're putting together a plan."

"But how can I reach him?" She was trembling, sick to her stomach, searching for an answer where none existed. The truth was more than she could take in. *My dad is a prisoner of war? What if someone's hurting him?* She shook her head, trying to clear her thoughts. "I have to talk to him."

"Shhh." Her mother ran her hand along the back of her head. "All we can do is wait. I'm sorry." Her voice cracked, and this was something else new: her mother allowing a show of emotion. She sniffed and held Hannah closer. "All we can do is wait."

❧

There was no word from the colonel by the next morning, so Hannah went to school. It was the only way she could make the time pass, the only way to keep running—the way that was familiar to her. But she couldn't concentrate on her classes or the lectures or anything but her father. There had to be something she could do, some way she could help him.

The idea came to her just after school let out. Her mother had a meeting with the congressman, looking for a way to speed up the rescue of her father and the men who had been with him on the mission. Hannah was skipping cheerleading, so she met Buddy Bingo out front near the flagpole at three o'clock. The temperatures hovered around freezing, and an icy wind hit her in the face as she flew out the school doors. More snow was in the forecast.

As soon as she climbed in the Town Car she leaned forward and craned her neck over the seat. "Buddy, I need help."

"What is it, Miss Hannah?" His eyes were instantly concerned.

She tugged on her sweater sleeves and explained the situation—how she had a different dad, one that she'd known as a little girl. And yesterday she'd found him, only he was overseas in Baghdad and now he was a prisoner of war. "He's in danger, Buddy." She gulped, terrified, too afraid to picture where he might be even at that minute. "You're praying for a Christmas miracle for me, right?"

"Right." Buddy's tone was gravely serious. "But Hannah, if he's a prisoner of war . . . has anyone heard from him?"

"That's just it." Her words came out fast, clipped. "His commander says they're putting together a rescue. So how about if we change the prayer and ask for a different miracle. That they'd find my dad and get him out of there before he gets hurt."

Buddy looked down and rubbed the back of his neck, slow and deliberate. When he looked up, he searched deep into her eyes. "Miss Hannah, can I ask you something?"

"Anything?" Hannah was out of breath. Her heart hadn't stopped racing since she saw the Town Car. If Buddy's miracle thing worked, then this might be her dad's only chance.

"Miracles aren't a given, Hannah. Do you know that?" Buddy's voice was serious.

"What do you mean?" She blinked; her heart skipped a beat. She needed a miracle now, more than ever.

"It takes belief, Hannah. Belief and prayer. Even so, sometimes God has another plan." He lowered his chin. "But either way, I can't be the only one believing and praying."

The notion hit Hannah square in the face. Buddy couldn't be the only one praying . . . of course not. She sat back and stared out the window. Why hadn't she thought of that before? Buddy was right. She could hardly ask him to pray for her Christmas miracle if she wasn't also willing to pray. She leaned up again and looked at him. "I do believe, Buddy. I've believed for a while now, I think. So . . ." She ran her tongue over her lower lip. "How do I pray?"

"There's no formula." Buddy gave her a familiar, tender smile, the one that made him look like Santa Claus. "You talk to God the same way you'd talk to your best friend."

"Can I try it?" Hannah tapped her toes on the floorboard of the car, the way she did when she was nervous. She looked around. They were still parked up against the curb in front of the school, but most of the other cars had already gone. "Right here?"

"Go ahead." Buddy bowed his head. "Give it a try."

Hannah followed his lead. She bowed her head and closed her eyes, more because it felt natural than because she was sure it was the right way to pray. She cleared her throat.

"Hi, God, it's me, Hannah." Her voice was shaky,

caught somewhere between scared-to-death for her father and uncertainty about what to say. She sucked in a quick breath. "God, my dad's in trouble. I haven't seen him in—" Her voice broke, and tears stung at her eyes.

"It's okay, Hannah." Buddy's voice was soft, low. "Take your time."

"Thanks." She swallowed a few times so she could find the words. She opened her eyes for a moment, and a trail of tears slid down both her cheeks. She sniffed and closed her eyes once more. "Anyway, God, I haven't seen my dad in a long time. And now he's a prisoner in Baghdad, and he needs your help. Remember the Christmas miracle Buddy's been praying for? That I would have Christmas with my mom and dad? Well—" The prayer was coming easier now. Buddy was right; it was just like talking. "—we'd like to add something. Please, God, just help Colonel Whalin and his men rescue my dad. That really would be the biggest, most amazing miracle of all. Thank You."

When she opened her eyes, Buddy was smiling at her. He held her gaze for a moment, then turned and pulled something out of a box on the seat next to him. It was a beautiful pair of red gloves—homemade, maybe. He held them out to her. "These are for you."

"Buddy . . ." She took them and turned them over, amazed at how soft they were. "Where did they come from?"

He turned so that he could see her straight on, see the

way the gloves fit her hands perfectly. "A long time ago, my mother gave me those." He pointed at the cuff on the gloves. "Look inside."

Hannah turned the cuff back and there, stitched on the inside in white, was the single word: *Believe.* She eased them onto her hands, one at a time, bringing them to her cheeks. "They're perfect."

"I've had them with me for a week or so." His eyes were bright, a mix of sadness and hope. "They're your Christmas present. But somehow"—he motioned to the gloves—"this seemed like the right time."

Hannah made her hands into fists and held her gloved fingers together. "Because of the message."

"Yes." Buddy patted her hands. "Because you need to believe. More now than ever."

"Thank you, Buddy." She felt warm all the way to her insides. "You always know what to say, what to do."

He took her home then, and she went inside to her room, to the quietest corner. There she took the gloves off and pressed them against her face. They smelled old, of cedar chests and cinnamon and long-ago Christmases. Already she treasured them. They would be a symbol, she decided. A reminder. She would wear them every time she left the house. That way she'd remember how important it was to pray.

And, when it came to miracles, how important it was to believe.

CHAPTER ELEVEN

The call Carol was dreading came Monday morning.

From the moment she'd heard that Mike was a prisoner of war, she'd been sick to her stomach. She was well aware of the treatment prisoners received in Iraq. Some were tortured and kept in cages, others were beaten and placed in pitch-dark solitary confinement. But ultimately, most of them were killed.

Hannah, meanwhile, walked around the house talking about prayer and belief and miracles, wearing a pair of red gloves the chauffeur had given her.

Carol had nothing against faith. If her daughter wanted to believe in something, fine. But believing in a miracle for her father couldn't possibly be wise. Not when he might already be dead.

Now, Hannah was at school when the phone rang. The knot in Carol's gut tightened as she took the call. "Hello?"

"Ms. Roberts?" It was Colonel Whalin's voice.

"Yes." Her heart rate doubled. "Do you have information about Hannah's father?"

The man was silent, and in that silence Carol knew. She knew that whatever news the commander was about to deliver would be bad—devastating, even. He cleared his voice. "We received an envelope from the insurgents."

Envelopes were never a good thing. Carol closed her eyes and waited.

"Inside were Mike's dog tags, the patches from his uniform—his name and rank—and a photo of a corpse." His voice was heavy. "I'm sorry, Ms. Roberts, as far as we can tell, the photo is of Hannah's father."

The bottom of Carol's heart fell away and she felt herself floating. *What will I tell Hannah?* How would her daughter ever forgive her for waiting so long to tell her about her dad? She pinched the bridge of her nose and forced herself to concentrate. "Are there identifying features, something that makes you sure it's him?"

"The body's dressed in a flight suit—one that appears to belong to Mike Meade."

Carol opened her eyes and stared out at the winter clouds. For a moment she saw him standing there, drenched in California sunshine, the surfboard beneath his arm. *"Come on, Carol, race you to the water!"* Her eyes stung. He was so strong, so vibrant and alive. She never should've kept Hannah from him, and now it was too late. She gave a shake of her head, searching for something to say. "Colonel Whalin . . ." How could he be gone? She massaged her throat. "What about the rescue?"

"It'll happen any day. From what we can tell nine men went down in the chopper and eight survived the crash, including Mike." He exhaled, his voice weary. "As many as seven of them may still be alive, trapped inside the insurgents' compound."

"Very well." She straightened herself, willing air to fill her lungs despite the panic suffocating her. "Please contact us afterward. Just in case."

"Yes." He paused, but in that pause there wasn't even a glimmer of hope. "Just in case."

✻✻✻

Hannah flew through the door just after three, the red gloves on her hands.

"Mother . . ." She was about to ask whether the colonel had called or not when she saw her mother's face. All her life, when she pictured her mother, Hannah had seen a dark-haired woman, beautiful and neatly put together. The image Carol Roberts gave to the world was not one that allowed shows of emotion or anything short of perfection.

That's how Hannah knew something was wrong.

As she rounded the corner into the living room, her mother was sitting on the sofa, her legs tucked beneath her. When she heard Hannah, she turned. Her face was streaked with mascara, her eyes swollen from crying. Her hair was flat and tucked behind her ears, as though she'd never even attempted to curl it.

"Mom?" Hannah stopped a few feet from her. She crossed her arms, cupping her elbows with her gloved hands. "What's wrong?"

"Hannah . . ." Her mother stood and shook her head. "I'm so sorry." Her eyes fell to the floor. "I should have told you about him sooner."

The thoughts in Hannah's head swirled and skipped around, and she struggled to make sense of her mother's statement. "Did . . ." She couldn't finish, couldn't bring herself to ask it. But she had no choice, because she had to know. Moving slow, carefully, she sat on the sofa arm, her eyes never left her mother's face. "Did the colonel call?"

Her mother lifted her head, her expression frozen, mouth drawn. "Yes." Her voice was so quiet, Hannah could hardly understand her. "They think your father's dead."

"No." Hannah shook her head, refusing to allow the words entrance to her mind. "No, Mother, he's a prisoner. He's not dead."

"Hannah," her mother stood and came to her. She looked tired and old and defeated. "His commander received an envelope with his things, his tags and patches, and a—" Her voice caught and she brought her hands to her face.

"What, Mother?" Hannah stood and went to her, taking hold of her wrists and lowering her hands so she could see her mother's face. But all the while she felt like a robot, as if her heart had been removed from her chest and she was merely operating on instinct. "What else?"

Her mother twisted her face, pain marking every crease and angle. She searched Hannah's eyes. "There was a photo of a dead man. They think . . . they think it's your father."

Hannah dropped her mother's hands. Her mouth hung open for a few moments, her mind racing. What had her mother said? They *thought* it was her father, right? Wasn't that it? They could be wrong, couldn't they? She swallowed, but her throat was too dry and the words wouldn't come.

Her knees shook and suddenly she couldn't stay on her feet another second. She dropped slowly to the ground, and somewhere in the distant places of her brain she heard herself begin to moan. "No . . . no, he can't be gone!"

"Hannah . . ." Her mother dropped to her knees next to her and put a hand on her back. "I'm so sorry."

"No!" She only shook her head, and this time the moan became louder, a desperate shout against everything that was happening around her, against the details that hung in the air like daggers over the two of them. She looked up and found her mother's eyes. "He could be wrong, couldn't he? The photo might not be my dad, right?"

It was her last hope, the last possibility that maybe— *maybe*—he was still alive, that the information was all some sort of terrible mistake. Her breathing was faster now, and she couldn't get enough air, couldn't seem to take a deep breath. Her chest heaved and she stared, wide eyed at her mother. "Right, Mom? Tell me I'm right!"

"Hannah . . ." Her mother shook her head, but that was all. There were no promises, no possibilities, nothing that would make her think for a moment that her mother held out any hope.

The red gloves felt like they were strangling her. Was this what she got for believing in miracles? A missed opportunity? A loss so great she couldn't fathom it? A father who never even knew how much she'd missed him? Was this what praying had brought about in her life?

She turned her hands palms up and was starting to tug on the fingers of the left glove when she spotted the word embroidered into the cuff: *Believe.* She stared at it and realized in a rush that already she'd stopped believing. In fact, she'd been about to throw the gloves across the room. Now, though, she froze, her eyes still on the word.

Next to her, her mother was saying something else, something about a rescue for whatever men might still be alive and how Colonel Whalin would call if there was any news, and suddenly Hannah gasped. "What did you say?"

Her mother slid over, closer. "Hannah, don't get your hopes up. Colonel Whalin saw the picture. It . . . it looked like your father."

"But they're doing a rescue, right?" She was on her feet, unable to contain the feelings welling within her. The gloves were only partway on her hands, and now she pushed her fingers hard back into them. No matter what, now, the gloves would stay. She lowered herself so her eyes were at the same level as her mother's. "A rescue, Mother, don't you see. The insurgents could've sent a bad picture. We won't know until they get all of the men out."

"I don't think it's smart to—"

"Please . . ." Hannah stood and touched her mother's shoulder with one red-gloved hand. "Give me this, Mother. I have to believe."

It was a truth she clung to the remainder of the day and through the night, when images of his capture and mistreatment threatened to suffocate her. Instead she prayed, just the way she'd done in Buddy Bingo's car.

Believing God could hear her, and that even now her father might still be alive. Believing it as though her next breath depended on it.

CHAPTER TWELVE

$\mathcal{T}$he cell where they had him locked was more of a cage, a four-by-four box with metal bars. Twice a day they opened the door, jerked him onto the floor outside the cell, blindfolded him, and took him outside. He could tell because of the wind and sand, and because of the sun that shone through even the thick cloth over his eyes.

It was the middle of the night, and near as Mike could tell, he'd been a prisoner for nearly a week.

The initial blows from his captors had knocked him out, but only for a few minutes. He came to as they were shoving him into the cell, and even then he pretended to be unconscious. Peering through swollen eyes he could see he was alone with his captors, no sign of the Rangers or his gunner. The moment he moved, the insurgents were on him, grabbing him from the cell, placing him in crude handcuffs and chaining him to a table. The questions came like machine-gun fire, in a sort of broken English that was common among the people of Iraq.

"What you name?"

Mike had set his jaw and spit out the information. He was allowed to tell his name, rank, and serial number. Nothing else.

In a matter of seconds, the questions got harder. "What you mission?"

The air in the room was stifling hot, dank and suffocating. There were no windows, and Mike had the feeling they were underground. He remained silent and looked away from the man who asked the question.

A chorus of angry shouts came at him in Iraqi. The man asking the questions took a step closer, grabbed Mike's chin, and jerked his face forward again. "You watch me," he said, his breath hot and stale. "Understand?"

Mike had no choice, not with his hands tied. He glared at his captor, studying him. His hair was longer than the others, and a scar ran across his right cheek.

"I ask again." His lips curled in a sneer. "What you mission?"

Whatever the consequence, Mike would never answer such a question. He'd given the insurgents all the information they would ever receive from him. He jerked hard enough so his chin broke free from the man's grip, and he was able to turn his head sharply left once more.

This time the man slapped him, sending his head forward with a jolt. He spit at Mike and when the men behind him chuckled, he shouted something in Iraqi at them. Then he looked at Mike once more. "I say tell me your mission."

The session had lasted for what felt like an hour. When they saw they could get no more information from him, the insurgents took turns kicking him. Finally the leader unchained him and pulled him to his feet. "You finished," he shouted at Mike. Then he yanked off every patch on Mike's flight suit. He leaned in so his nose was touching Mike's. His voice dropped to a whisper. "You dead soldier."

The man's tone had left no doubt. Mike closed his eyes, but instead of imagining the bullet that would certainly slice through him any moment, he put himself in another place—the place he'd put himself for the past eleven years. On Pismo Beach with Hannah at his side, the smell of salt water filling his senses, the sun hot on his back as they worked on a sandcastle.

He could hear her little-girl laughter, feel her hand on his arm as she clamored for his attention every few minutes. *"Look, Daddy . . . a new shell!"* or *"See, Daddy . . . it has a door now!"*

But the bullet never came.

Instead, the leader grabbed his arm and shoved him onto the floor. "Crawl, soldier!"

And Mike did. He shuffled forward on his knees and when he was near the cell door, the man kicked him hard enough to send him crashing into the backside of the metal bars. The man locked the door, shouted something Mike didn't understand, and then the group of them left him alone.

Mike hadn't taken a full breath until they were gone. He was handcuffed, but he brought his fingers to his face and covered his eyes, unable to believe they'd let him live.

That was six days ago. The men—with different ones acting as the leader—had repeated the questioning every few hours since then, always with death threats. Once they showed him a photo of a headless corpse, and the leader from the first day gave him an evil smile. "That will be you, soldier. Soon."

Mike still believed it was true, but after surviving the first day, he began to do something he hadn't done in years. He began to pray. Back at the base, Stoker was praying for him. He had no doubts. He might as well pray for himself. The confinement was tight and cramped and lonely, and if nothing else, praying gave him someone to talk to. He believed in God, believed there was a purpose to life and the people who came and left from it.

At least that's the way he saw it that first night. But trapped in the cell, his body cramping from the heat and lack of water, certain that death was hours away, talking to God became a life rope, a desperate cry from the depths of darkness. And all because he wanted the one thing he'd wanted since he'd enlisted.

The chance to see Hannah again.

Mike brought his cuffed hands to the cell bars and

gripped them. He could hear the scurrying of a mouse—or what he figured were mice, but what might've also been cockroaches. The sound had been constant since they locked him up. But now, no matter how hard he tried to peer into the darkness, he couldn't see a thing. Nothing.

"God . . . I know You can see me, even here." He whispered the prayer out loud this time. Hearing his own voice on occasion helped him stay focused. Because even though the situation seemed dismal, he had to believe he was getting out, that his captors would forget him outside one of these times or leave him at the interrogating table unwatched. Something so that he could get away.

He tried again. "I know You're here, God. Talk to me, be with me." He tightened his grip on the bars. "Get me out of here. Please. Let me find Hannah."

No audible voice answered him in return, but something strange happened. The scurrying in the background stopped. It stopped for the next few minutes, and there was only the sound of his heartbeat. He relaxed his hands some. "God?"

He waited another few minutes and still the silence remained, and something more. A sense of peace, a knowledge that he wasn't in control but that God certainly was. No other way to explain it. He settled back onto the floor of the cage and leaned against the bars.

Whether he was there for ten minutes or two hours, he couldn't tell, but suddenly there was a shattering sound and the rapid explosion of gunfire. Before he could process what was happening, the room filled with light and three Army Rangers tore into it.

"Identify yourself," one of them shouted.

"Captain Mike Meade, U.S. Army."

"You're alive!" The lead Ranger snapped the lock on the small cell. "We have to move fast."

"I'll keep up." Mike could barely breathe. He was being rescued? Was that what was happening? Or was he dreaming, barely holding onto his sanity?

"There's no time." The first Ranger helped him out of the cell. "You all right?"

He ducked until he was clear of the bars, and then stood up. "Fine." Questions could come later. "Let's go."

They raced across the dirt floor and up a flight of stairs. As they were running another round of shouts rang out, followed by a quick string of bullets. Mike's heart pounded in his throat, but he had no time to think, no time to analyze whether it was all a dream or not.

When they reached the outside, he tore around the corner, close behind the Rangers. The loud pulsing of a helicopter made it impossible to hear anything. Where were the others, his gunner and the Rangers who'd been on his chopper? From the corner of his eye he saw bodies on the ground and for half a second he turned to look. The insurgents—it must have been them. All dead. His men must've already been rescued. Mike gulped, faced straight ahead again, and picked up his pace.

"Hurry!" One of the Rangers shouted above the sound of the helicopter.

Mike moved faster, keeping up with the soldiers even though his muscles were cramping, his lungs burning inside his chest. He had barely moved in a week. Now he was running on adrenaline, step after step, closer to escape. *God . . . is this real? Did You hear me?*

He blinked and gave a few shakes of his head. Whatever it was, he had to keep moving. Four more steps, five, six, and there she was. Hannah, standing in front of him, twirling in her first princess nightgown. *"You're my best friend, Daddy. Right?"*

"Faster, move it!" The Ranger's voice snapped him to attention.

Mike pushed his feet through the sand, one after the other, again and again. Ahead of him, an Army helicopter hovered over the roof of the building, not far from the place where he had attempted to hover a week earlier. A rope dangled from an open door, and the first Ranger grabbed it and shimmied up. Mike was next, but he didn't need help. He was in the chopper in record time, his sides heaving.

"I'll contact Colonel Whalin," one of the rangers said to another.

And only then did Mike know one thing without a doubt.

He wasn't dreaming.

❧

$\mathcal{T}$he chopper flew to Baghdad International Airport and after an hour of debriefing with military personnel in a private area, Colonel Whalin entered the room. He stopped short when he saw Mike. His steps slowed, and their eyes locked.

When his commander reached him, Mike stood at attention. "Sir, the mission . . ." Emotions that Mike hadn't known before swelled in his chest. *Where are my men?* He coughed, working the words free. "The mission failed."

"Yes, Meade." Colonel Whalin's eyes were steely, but they glistened. "At ease."

Mike exhaled and let himself fall against a wall. They'd fed him and given him a sports drink to help hydrate him faster. But still he felt weak, overwhelmed. "I'm . . . sorry, sir."

"Meade, it wasn't your fault." The colonel looked Mike straight in the eyes. "You've gotta believe that."

He didn't want to ask the next question. "The others? They must've gotten out first?"

"No." An angry sigh came from the colonel. He raked his hand across the back of his head and let out an angry sigh. "Meade, I don't know how to tell you this."

Somewhere above his ankles, Mike felt himself begin to tremble. *No . . . It can't be . . .* "They did get out, sir." He searched his commander's face. "Tell me they got out."

Colonel Whalin pursed his lips, stared up at the ceiling, and gave a quick few shakes of his head. When he looked at Mike, there was no mistaking this time. His eyes were full of unshed tears. "We lost them all, Meade. All of them. Insurgents shot them before they ever made it into the building." He cursed under his breath. "It was a setup, Meade. A bad tip. No one should've made it out alive."

Mike felt faint, his head dizzy. They were gone? All the men on the mission? Why would their captors kill everyone but him? Then slowly it began to make sense. He was in charge; he had the information they wanted. The insurgents would've viewed the others as . . . dispensable.

He bent at his waist and gripped his knees. His breathing was different, more shallow. He couldn't get enough air no matter what he tried. *Deep breaths,* he told himself. *Slow, deep breaths.* He craned his neck back and looked at the colonel again. "I should've died with them, sir. The way it ended . . . it isn't right."

"You're wrong, Meade." Colonel Whalin searched Mike's face. "You followed orders."

"Sir?" Mike blinked. His head was still cloudy, his mind unclear. He could see his team in the chopper as they crossed enemy lines, CJ at his side, the gunner and the Rangers ready for action. Now they were gone, all of them. He blinked the memory back. "What orders, sir?"

"My orders, Meade. I told you to come back alive."

The colonel coughed, but his chin quivered. "You did what I asked."

Mike's throat was too thick to speak. There was nothing more to say, nothing he could add. The reasons weren't clear, they'd never be clear, but he was here, alive. His commander was right.

The debriefing lasted another few hours. When they were finished, Colonel Whalin lit a Camel and lifted a piece of paper from the desk in the room. "We have a plan for you, Meade. We're getting you home as quick as possible."

"Thank you, sir." Mike gripped his knees and tried to make sense of everything that was happening. His co-pilot was dead, the gunner, the Rangers, everyone else on the chopper. But here he was getting special treatment, a quicker trip back to the U.S. Probably so he could be home for Christmas. As if he might have any reason to be home.

Colonel Whalin was going on about the trip home, explaining that he would be placed on a C-130 Hercules cargo plane for a five-hour flight to Ramstein Air Base in Frankfurt, Germany. From there he'd fly on a C-17, a bigger cargo aircraft, back to the States.

"I pulled some strings." The colonel's face was still shadowed by the seriousness of the situation. "You got a nonstop to Andrews Air Force Base."

"Andrews?" That airport was more than a day's drive from his base. "I'm flying to Maryland?"

"It's Christmas, Meade. I figured you'd want to be with your daughter."

It took several heartbeats before he could fully process the statement. His daughter? *Hannah?* What would Colonel Whalin know about her? He rubbed the back of his head and stood, gripping the edge of the desk. "Colonel, I haven't seen my daughter in eleven years."

"You said you were expecting her call?" The colonel cocked his head, curious. "That's the same daughter, right?"

Mike breathed out. He hadn't told anyone in the service about Hannah, not ever. "I have one daughter, sir. Her mother took her from me when I enlisted. I haven't heard from her or seen her since."

The colonel leaned forward and slammed his elbows on the desk. "How'd you know she might call?"

"A video. It's a long story." This time Mike's heart stopped. "Wait . . . she called?" He straightened, his mouth open. By the time his heart kicked in he found his voice again. "Hannah called? At your office?"

"She lives in the outskirts of Washington, D.C. I have all the information." For the first time that day, the colonel smiled.

"That's why I'm flying to Andrews, sir?"

"Now you're getting it, Meade. I thought you'd like to spend Christmas with your daughter. The way the flights worked out, you should be there Christmas Eve."

Mike felt something strange and unfamiliar, a bursting in his heart, a giddiness that spread through him, along his limbs all the way to his hands and feet. Hannah had called? She'd talked with his commander? How was it even possible? Hours earlier he was locked in a cage, death raging around him, and now here he was. Every dream he'd ever had, about to come true.

He closed his eyes. *God . . . You did this, didn't You?*

In light of the future that lay ahead of him, the horror of the past week faded a little. And suddenly he realized what he was feeling, the amazing sensation making its way through him. It was something he hadn't felt for years.

Pure, uninhibited joy.

EPILOGUE

$\mathcal{H}$annah still wore the gloves.

She had nothing if she didn't have hope, and somehow the red gloves reminded her she could still pray, still believe. It was Christmas Eve, and she hadn't moved too far from the phone all day. Her mother had given up. She was busy in the office making calls to Sweden. Whenever she passed by, she would pat Hannah on the shoulder and give her a sad smile, as if to say everything would be okay, the sorrow would pass in time.

Hannah would only shake her head. "Mother, don't look at me like that. He's okay, I can feel it. I won't quit believing that until he comes home."

Her mother would hesitate and move on to some other order of business. There was always an order of business, and for her the order of finding Mike Meade was over.

But it wasn't over. Hannah refused to believe it. She'd

prayed, and Buddy Bingo had told her that God heard everything. And if God had heard her, then somehow she'd get to see her dad again, right?

Hannah walked into the front room and stared out the window. It was snowing again, the way it had been all day. The fireplace was alive, the flames dancing merrily, unaware of the trouble her father was in. She moved closer and turned one of the chairs so it faced the fire.

What else had Buddy said? That miracles weren't a given?

That idea was the one she couldn't allow to take root, because then she'd have to believe it was possible—after not knowing about him for so many years, now he might really be gone.

She sat down and faced the fire. "God . . . where is he?"

Her cheeks were cold, and she lifted her gloved hands to her face. The question floated in the air like the clouds outside. In the flames she could see him, his face the way it looked in the picture, the way it looked in her long ago memories. She was still thinking about him, still remembering, when she heard a knock at the door.

The house staff was off for the day, and her mother and grandmother were upstairs. She stood, stretched, and went to the foyer. They weren't expecting anyone, so maybe it was a delivery. They delivered on Christmas Eve, didn't they? If presents needed to get somewhere, right?

She opened the door. "Hello?"

On the step stood a man dressed in Army gear. In his hand he held a worn-looking paper sack. Something about him was familiar, and for half a second she wondered if he was her father. But that was impossible. He might be alive, but he was in Iraq, not Washington, D.C. Whoever the man was, his cheeks were red and he stared at her like he was seeing a ghost.

Just then she had a sudden fear and she took two steps backward. What if he'd come on official Army business, to tell her that her father was dead? Would the Army do that to her? On Christmas Eve? She took another step back. "Can . . . can I help you?"

He didn't look at her, he looked through her. And the "something familiar" was more so all the time. Then he swallowed and said, "Hannah?"

Her heart beat faster than before. "Yes?" Why did he look at her that way? Was this how it happened? How families found out that someone they loved was gone? She wanted to close her eyes and make him go away, but it was too late. The conversation had already begun. Now she'd have to see it through.

Then, the Army man's eyes welled with tears. He swallowed and took a step forward. "Hannah . . . I'm your father."

Her body shook and she felt dizzy, so dizzy she had to grab the doorframe to keep from falling. "Dad?" How could he be here? He was supposed to be in Iraq, a prisoner of war. His commander thought he was dead, right?

She blinked, trying to make sense of what she was seeing. "How could . . . I can't believe it." Her voice faded to nothing before she finished the sentence.

"Look at you, Hannah." A tear rolled down one of his cheeks. "You're all grown up."

And suddenly she knew it was him, knew it because the eyes were the same as the ones in the photographs. But more than that, they were the eyes from her memory. In a rush she ran to him. Her red-gloved hands went around his waist and she pressed her cheek to his chest. "I never forgot you, Daddy."

He shook against her, and Hannah could tell he was crying. They stayed that way for a while, holding on as if by doing so they could somehow find the years they'd lost. When he finally drew back a little, he searched her eyes. "I looked for you every chance I had." He held out the brown paper sack. "I kept this with me."

Hannah took the fragile bag and opened it. From inside she pulled out a folded piece of paper. She handed the bag back to her dad and opened the sheet. It was tattered and creased, but clearly it was a picture she'd drawn for her father. Across the top she'd written *Hannah loves Daddy.*

In an instant the memory came back. She was sitting at a small table, her father across from her. They were both coloring, weren't they? And hers had been a drawing of the two of them, her and her father, complete with their oversized silly grins and the big sun ball in the sky.

A picture of everything life had been for the two of them. Smiles and sunshine and togetherness.

She folded it carefully, handed it to her father, and met his eyes. "I remember making it for you."

"Really?" He slipped the paper back into the bag. "You really remember me?"

Hannah sniffed and tried to find her voice. Her tears were becoming sobs as the moment became more real. This was him, her father. The man she'd been missing for eleven years. "Yes." She grabbed a quick breath. "I remember you playing with me on the floor and . . . and reading to me." She took hold of his hands, feeling the warmth of his fingers through the red gloves. "I remember you playing the guitar." She put her arms around him again and pressed her cheek against his chest. "You must've seen my message."

"I did." He stroked her hair. "I couldn't believe it was you. After so many years of looking."

"They told us . . ." She swallowed a series of sobs. "They told us you were dead."

He tightened his hold on her. "I should be."

She drew back and studied his face. Whatever he'd been through, it must've been horrible. "Look at this." She held up her gloved hands, and turned the cuff down so he could read the embroidered word written on the inside of each.

"Believe." His voice was quiet, amazed.

She thought of Buddy Bingo, praying every day for her

Christmas miracle. Her tears subsided, and she caught her breath. "A friend gave them to me." She looked at the inside of the cuffs, and then up to her dad. "I wore them because I believed you'd be okay, that they'd rescue you, and you'd call." She made a sound that was mostly laughter. "I never thought you'd show up on my doorstep!"

He peered around her. "Can I come in?"

The question was a serious one; Hannah could see that in her father's eyes. After all, her mother had left without a forwarding address. He wouldn't know whether she'd want him in their house, even after so many years.

"Of course." Hannah hurried back a few steps and ushered him inside. "Mother's been helping me find you. She'll be so glad you're okay."

They made their way inside by the fire and sat in opposite chairs, their hands joined in the middle. Hannah told him about her life, how her mother had married a politician and how she rarely saw either of them.

"I'm sorry, Hannah." His shoulders slumped. "That's not right."

She shrugged. "It's all I know."

"Not after today." He flexed the muscles in his jaw. "I'm never leaving you."

There were steps in the foyer and then in the hallway, and she could hear her mother's voice. "Hannah? Is someone here?"

The look of perfection was back, and as her mother stepped into the room she was the picture of poise and position. Her eyes moved from Hannah to her father, and she came to a slow stop. "Mike?"

He stood and went to her, stopping short of a hug. She reached out her hands and he took them as their eyes locked onto each other. "Carol. You're still beautiful." He smiled, but Hannah could see the pain in his eyes.

"They told us you were dead." She looked at Hannah. "Did you tell him?"

"Yes, Mother." She stood, amazed at what she was seeing.

Her dad said something else then, something about being rescued and getting a rushed trip back home, but Hannah wasn't really listening. Her heart was in her throat. She'd found her daddy, the man in her memories. And now, whatever happened after this, she wasn't letting him go. He would be a part of her life forever more. Wasn't that what he'd said?

God had brought him home to her on Christmas Eve. She could hardly wait to tell Buddy. And what would her grandmother say? What would her daddy and her mother have to say to each other, once they got past these first few minutes?

That's when Hannah realized what had happened. Not only because her father was standing before her, but because her mother was, too. The thing she'd wanted most of all was her father's rescue, and that she might spend Christmas with her parents. Now, against any reason or commonsense, she was going to do just that.

A smile lifted the corners of her mouth and she studied her father, proud of him. He was a captain, a chopper pilot. And there he was, tall and strong and bigger than life! A song rang out from the depths of her soul. Because she could imagine getting to know her dad again, and maybe living with him when her mother was out of the country. Maybe singing while he played the guitar, or taking a trip to Pismo Beach with him so he could teach her to surf. She could imagine all of it, a life with her dad the way she'd always known it could be.

And that was something so big, so amazing, Buddy Bingo was right.

It could only be a Christmas miracle.

AUTHOR'S NOTE

*H*ello friends!

Merry Christmas, and thanks for traveling with me through the pages of yet another Red Gloves novel. It's become part of my pre–Christmas tradition, writing these stories and bringing them to you, knowing that for many of you they are now a part of your traditions as well.

If this is your first Red Gloves novel, let me give you a little background. In the book *Gideon's Gift* I told the story of a sick little girl and an angry homeless man and the gift that changes both their lives forever. That gift was a pair of red gloves. In the back of that book, I listed service project ideas—Red Gloves Projects. The goal was that you would travel from the pages of the story to the streets of your community, where you and your family or friends or coworkers might do something to help the homeless.

Next came *Maggie's Miracle,* with Red Gloves Projects

for needy children, and *Sarah's Song,* with Red Gloves Projects for the elderly. Always the red gloves play a cameo role in the story, bringing to mind again the gift Gideon gave to old, angry Earl in the first Red Gloves novel.

Hannah's Hope, of course, is a story centered around an earnest teenager who wants desperately to be reunited with her military father. The fact is around our country today there are thousands of children who feel the same way Hannah did. Not because they've been separated from their parents by thoughtlessness, the way Hannah was. Rather, because war has separated them.

Because of this, and to bring honor to the men and women who serve this country through the U.S. Armed Services, this year's Red Gloves Projects will center around the military. Our family started a Red Gloves Project for the military a few years ago. When we're in an airport, whenever we see a uniformed soldier, we slip him or her a twenty-dollar bill. Then we tell him or her, "Thank you for defending our freedom. Have lunch on us."

My kids and I did that last January at O'Hare International Airport. One of the uniformed soldiers was a tentative-looking young man standing in a food line with an older man who appeared to be his father. We gave him the money and the thank you and returned to our table.

A few minutes later, the young man's father approached us. He had tears in his eyes. "My son is going back for a second tour in Iraq." He held out his chest, clearly proud of his boy. "We would've been tempted to feel pretty low today." He paused. "You will never know how much your gift meant to us."

My kids and I were left with a joy that is indescribable. The simple joy of giving the gift of hope and appreciation to someone who deserves it.

With that in mind, I bring you this year's Red Gloves Projects:

RED GLOVES PROJECTS

🌿 By networking through your church or school or workplace, identify two to four soldiers currently serving overseas. Make a plan to bring them as much joy and appreciation as possible this Christmas. Round up as many people as you can, and have them write thank-you letters to the soldiers. You might contact your local school or organize this through your place of employment. Letters from both children and adults would be best. Next, purchase something special to go with the letters. Soldiers tell me that chewing gum and jelly beans are especially nice in the dusty desert areas. Finally, pack the letters and gifts in a box and top it off with a pair of Red Gloves and a copy of *Hannah's Hope* or another Christmas story whose message you enjoy. You might consider multiple copies so the soldier can pass them out to his or her friends. Reading material is hard to come by.

❦ Contact your local Armed Services recruiting office and ask if there are any soldiers who will not have the finances to come home for Christmas. Organize a group of people willing to help in this matter. Stage a fundraiser, or have these people donate money to the cause. Then arrange with the local office to purchase airfare for that soldier. Make sure you know the date and time he or she will be returning. Plan for your group to be at the airport with signs that read, "Welcome Home," and "Thank you!"

❦ Some soldiers will not have time off during Christmas. This will be an emotional burden on their families, but it can also be a financial strain. Talk to the local Armed Services office again, and ask if there are soldiers whose families could benefit from donated gifts. If so, get a group together and purchase those gifts. Deliver them with letters to the families, thanking them for sacrificing time with their loved ones so that we can remain a free country.

❦ Using the method in the first idea, locate a soldier who has family in your area. Next contact the soldier and express an interest in letting his or her entire unit know how grateful you are for their service. In our area, third-grade teacher Kathy Santschi arranged a campaign called "Jelly Bellies for Jonathan." Jonathan Vansandt is a friend of ours, and he had expressed a general wish in his unit for Jelly Bellies. All told, Kathy Santschi's third graders collected well over a hundred pounds of Jelly Bellies. Jonathan was the recipient, but he shared Jelly Bellies with dozens of soldiers serving in Iraq alongside him. The candy came with letters from the children, and Jonathan says it lifted the spirits of the entire unit for weeks. You could do this sort of thing with chewing gum or inspirational novels or whatever you think might change the course of a few weeks for an entire unit of soldiers.

Of course, the one thing we can all do for our men and women serving overseas is pray. Make a prayer calendar with your family or group, and choose to deliberately pray for those serving in all branches of the Armed Forces. Pray for our president and the decisions he must make in the fight for freedom. And pray that God's mighty hand of protection be over everyone fighting for freedom across the world.

You may not have twenty dollars for every soldier you see in an airport or at a supermarket this Christmas. But make a point of going up and shaking his or her hand. Look that soldier in the eyes and be clear about how thankful you are. You never know. Your words of thanks might make all the difference.

Author's Note

$\mathscr{I}$pray you have a wonderful, joyous Christmas season, finding time with friends and family, and making special note of the moments together. The years fly quickly, and what we celebrate today will tomorrow be but a memory. Please contact me at my e-mail address, rtnbykk@aol.com, and tell me about your Red Gloves Projects. They are happening around the world now. If we all do our part to experience the joy of giving, together we truly can put Christ back into our Christmas celebration.

Until next time, in His light and love,

Karen Kingsbury

P.S. I'd love to hear from you, as always.
www.KarenKingsbury.com

A NOTE FROM THE EDITORS

$\mathcal{W}$e hope you enjoyed *Hannah's Hope* by Karen Kingsbury, published by the Books and Inspirational Media Division of Guideposts, a nonprofit organization that touches millions of lives every day through products and services that inspire, encourage, help you grow in your faith, and celebrate God's love.

Thank you for making a difference with your purchase of this book, which helps fund our many outreach programs to military personnel, prisons, hospitals, nursing homes, and educational institutions.

We also create many useful and uplifting online resources. Visit Guideposts.org to read true stories of hope and inspiration, access OurPrayer network, sign up for free newsletters, download free e-books, join our Facebook community, and follow our stimulating blogs.

To learn about other Guideposts publications, including the best-selling devotional *Daily Guideposts*, go to Guideposts. org/Shop, call (800) 932-2145, or write to Guideposts, PO Box 5815, Harlan, Iowa 51593.